"You're shivering. Are you cold?" Jon's gaze lifted to her face. "No, you're not cold . . ."

"No," Elizabeth whispered. Heat was throbbing through every vein. She could feel the flush on her cheeks and throat.

He closed his eyes. "Not now. Don't do this to me now. I thought I had it under control . . ." His eyes opened. Burning. Brilliant. Hungry."

"Do you suppose you could just hold me?" she asked softly.

His eyes were smoky and glazed as he looked at her. "Yes, I can do that. It's going to come close to killing me, but I can do it." Jon's mouth was moving closer and she could feel his warm breath on her lips. His arms tightened around her and pulled her against his chest. She wanted to bury her fingers in his hair and bring him even closer to her.

His lips covered hers then, and a shudder ran through her. She gasped against his mouth, as if his touch had jerked hot cords somewhere within her. She opened her lips in a low cry. The sensation was indescribable: his mouth hard, yet gentle, caressing her own. She was lost in the intimacy of the kiss, knowing she'd never before shared so much, given so much of herself through the simple yet passionate act of kissing . . .

Bantam Books by Iris Johansen
Ask your bookseller for the titles you have missed

WHAT ARE *LOVESWEPT* ROMANCES?

They are stories of true romance and touching emotion. We believe those two very important ingredients are constants in our highly sensual and very believable stories in the *LOVESWEPT* line. Our goal is to give you, the reader, stories of consistently high quality that may sometimes make you laugh, sometimes make you cry, but are always fresh and creative and contain many delightful surprises within their pages.

Most romance fans read an enormous number of books. Those they truly love, they keep. Others may be traded with friends and soon forgotten. We hope that each *LOVESWEPT* romance will be a treasure—a "keeper." We will always try to publish

LOVE STORIES YOU'LL NEVER FORGET
BY AUTHORS YOU'LL ALWAYS REMEMBER

The Editors

LOVESWEPT® • 187

Iris Johansen
Last Bridge Home

BANTAM BOOKS
TORONTO • NEW YORK • LONDON • SYDNEY • AUCKLAND

LAST BRIDGE HOME

A Bantam Book / April 1987

*LOVESWEPT® and the wave device are registered
trademarks of Bantam Books, Inc. Registered in U.S. Patent
and Trademark Office and elsewhere.*

*If you would be interested in receiving protective vinyl
covers for your Loveswept books, please write to this address
for information:*

Loveswept
Bantam Books
P.O. Box 985
Hicksville, NY 11802

ISBN 0-553-21814-X

Published simultaneously in the United States and Canada

PRINTED IN THE UNITED STATES OF AMERICA

O   0 9 8 7 6 5 4 3 2 1

One

The gray Ford sedan wasn't parked on the tree-shadowed side road today.

Elizabeth Ramsey loosened her white-knuckled grip on the steering wheel as she slowed her car. She sighed with relief. She hadn't realized how tightly she had been clutching the wheel until the tension suddenly flowed out of her like air rushing from a pricked balloon.

Stupid. She was being so incredibly stupid. She'd only seen the car parked there four times. It was possible there was no one in the car. Perhaps the driver was a hunter or someone as innocuous as a bird watcher. She had never felt afraid before on this lonely stretch of road, which led to Mill Cottage. It had just been the way home. The road she loved most in the entire world.

It must be pregnant lady's nerves, she decided with a grimace. She had never thought she would be prone to this sort of weakness, but she had learned she wasn't nearly as pragmatic as she had once believed in the eight months since Mark had died and . . . She firmly blocked the thought before it could take root and flourish as the familiar barbs of pain. Think about the baby. The baby. Don't think about Mark or the past.

Her hand left the steering wheel to rest on the taut swelling of her stomach through the cotton of her loose blue shirt. Life. Soon. All she had to do was hold on a little longer, and then the loneliness would be over for both of them. There was a slight movement beneath her palm and her lips curved in a warm smile of delight. It was almost as if Andrew had read her thoughts and was trying to reassure her.

The tender smile still lingered on her lips as her hand returned to the steering wheel. Maybe this imagining business wasn't so bad after all. Not if it brought comfort as well as those silly spurts of panic. She had been foolish to worry.

She speeded up as she drove into the old covered bridge and the familiar rumble of the planks beneath the tires of her station wagon murmured a soothing chant of the homecoming that was just beyond the next turn in the road. She left the bridge, negotiated the serpentine curve, and Mill Cottage came into view. She immediately felt a surge of peace and reassurance. The ivy-covered stone cottage was very old and had a serenity about it which was rarely found in modern architecture. From her seat in the car, she could see the ancient oak paddle wheel that had powered the mill and furnished the first American Cart-wrights with their livelihood. The wheel was still now, and no longer churned the waters of the smooth silver stream winding through the meadow and into the distant woods. Most of the trees in the woods were bare, only the pines retained their greenery. She shivered, and looked once again at the cottage. Home. Inviting, welcoming, warmth in a world that would soon know winter. She rounded the last bend in the road, and the drive-way of the cottage appeared before her.

She inhaled sharply as she spotted a man stand-ing on the stone steps at the front door of the cottage. A man she had never seen before. Imme-diately her gaze flew to the car parked in the driveway. It was a dark green pickup truck, not a gray Ford sedan.

She pulled her car into the driveway and slowed it to a stop. Nerves or no nerves, it wouldn't hurt to be cautious. She kept her windows rolled up and the doors locked. The man, who was coming down the steps now, didn't look menacing, but he didn't look like the Caspar Milquetoast type either. There was something very controlled about his deliberate approach. Controlled. What an odd word to come to mind, she thought. His deeply tanned face was completely impassive, yet she had the impression he was exerting a tremendous ef-fort to subdue forces that were seething below the surface of his calm exterior.

Standing beside her window, he bent down slightly to look at her. He spoke in a tone a level above normal so she could hear through the glass. "I'm glad you're being cautious. It's very lonely out here for a woman alone. I've been waiting for you."

He was gazing at her with an odd, almost hungry, intentness. The thought that he was only inches away, separated from her by a flimsy sheet of glass, sent a sudden shudder of fear through her. His eyes were darkly brilliant, his black brows heavy, and his bone structure was too strongly defined to ever be termed handsome. Strength. A strength so powerful it was a shock to her senses. She found herself staring at him in wide-eyed fascination.

He frowned. "For God's sake, stop looking at me like that." His voice was rough and slightly husky. "I'm not going to hurt you. I'm here to help you. I'd never—" He broke off and drew a deep breath. "Look, I'm sorry if I startled you. Let's begin again. My name is Jon Sandell and Mark Ramsey was my cousin. Perhaps he mentioned me?"

Jon Sandell. She felt a swift swell of relief and hurriedly rolled down the window. "Of course he did. I'm very glad to meet you at last." She grinned and wrinkled her nose at him. "Though you probably think I'm flighty as a loon to treat you as if you were Charles Manson. I'm not usually this uptight. I guess I have a case of prenatal jitters." She opened the door and swung her khaki-clad legs carefully to the ground. It was a massive undertaking for her to get herself out from behind the steering wheel these days. Jon Sandell stepped forward and lifted her easily from the seat and onto her feet.

"Oh, thank you, that helped a lot. I'll be with

you in just a minute. I have to get the groceries out of the car. I stopped at the supermarket on the way home from school, which delayed me a bit. Have you been waiting long?"

"No." He was frowning again. "You shouldn't be out here by yourself. It may have been all right before, but now that you're—"

"—big as a house," she finished for him. She shut the car door and went around to the back of the station wagon. "This is my home. Where else would I go?" She unlocked and opened the gate. "Besides, I'm not alone. The Spauldings have a farm two miles down the road, and I have Sam."

He stiffened. "Sam?"

She gazed at him in puzzlement. Why was he so disturbed? Then the answer came to her. Mark had said Jon Sandell was the only family he possessed. They must have been very close. It was only natural that Mark's cousin would be upset to find out there was another man in her life only eight months after Mark's death.

"Sam is my Heinz 57," she said with a gentle smile. "He's half Great Dane and half I-don't-know-what. I'm surprised you haven't seen him. I let him run loose while I'm at school."

"You're still attending the university in Albany?" he asked as he stopped her from reaching for the grocery bags. A small amount of tension seemed to have disappeared from his demeanor. "You go on inside. It's cold out here now that the sun's gone down. I'll bring these in."

"You'll stay for dinner? I put a stew in the Crockpot this morning. There will be plenty for two."

He shook his head. "I can't stay but I'd like a cup of coffee and a little conversation, if it's not too much trouble."

She shook her head as she turned and headed for the steps. "Of course it's not too much trouble. I'd like to talk to you too." She glanced back over her shoulder as she unlocked the heavy Dutch door. A smile lit her face with glowing warmth, and she said, "Mark was a stranger in these parts and not many people got to know him well enough to realize how wonderful he was. I think one of the things I missed most after he died was not being able to talk to someone who loved him as much as I did."

He was gazing at her face with the same intent expression she had noticed earlier. "I wanted to come to you then, but they wouldn't let me."

"I understood why you couldn't come to the funeral. Mark had told me you are out of the country most of the time."

He reached in the wagon for a grocery sack. "That's a fairly accurate way of phrasing it. Well, I'm here now. Why don't you go inside."

His last words were a command, spoken with the casual confidence of someone accustomed to being obeyed. Whoever "they" were, they must have been exceptionally high up in the echelon of Sandell's company to prevent him from doing anything he wanted to do. She saluted. "I'll put the coffee on, sir."

He looked up, and for the flicker of a moment there was a warm smile on his hard face. "Was I being authoritarian? I was in the military for a while and I guess you never really lose a sense of command."

She should have realized Sandell was a military man. He certainly looked the part, she thought. His shoulders were broad and powerful beneath the brown plaid of his mackinaw, and he moved with crisp precision.

"I guess you don't." She swung open the door and left it ajar for him as she moved briskly down the hall to the large kitchen which stretched the length of the rear of the cottage.

Switching on the light, she hurried over to the counter and plugged in the coffee maker, which she had readied before she had left that morning. Then she knelt and touched a lighted match to the kindling in the brick fireplace, watching with satisfaction as the fire sprang cozily to life. It was her routine to have all the preparations for the evening out of the way when she walked out the door in the morning. She had discovered early in her pregnancy that by the time she put in a full day at school, she was often too tired for anything but a bath and bed.

"If you'll tell me where things go in the cupboard, I'll put them away for you." Jon Sandell was standing in the doorway with three bags balanced in his arms.

"I'll put them away later, just set them on the counter." She took the plastic bag containing the items that needed refrigeration, and crossed the parquet floor to the Coppertone refrigerator against the wall. "You can get cups and saucers from the cupboard to your left, if you like. Do you use milk or sugar?"

"No."

"Neither do I." She put the eggs, milk, and butter into the refrigerator. "I like my coffee black as sin and loaded with caffeine. I've been drinking it without caffeine lately because it's better for the baby, but I still miss the pick-me-up it gave me." One hand absently rubbed the hollow of her spine as she closed the refrigerator door. "And weighing as much as I do these days, it takes a heck of a lot to pick me u—" She broke off as she turned to face him. "You're looking at me very oddly. Is something wrong?"

"No." He looked away as he took two cups and saucers from the cupboard shelf. "I was just thinking how beautiful you are."

She laughed with genuine amusement. "I'm not even pretty. Lord, you *must* have been out of the country and away from civilization and women for a long time. Where were you anyway? In the wilds of the Sahara? Remind me to introduce you to my neighbor, Serena Spaulding. She's simply gorgeous."

She took the coffee carafe and crossed the room to where he was standing. "But thanks anyway for trying to make a fat, pregnant lady feel good." She poured the steaming liquid into the cups and turned to set the carafe on the warmer. "Take off your coat and sit down." She shrugged out of her heavy navy peacoat. "I'll be right back. I have to call Sam and tell him it's chow time."

"I wouldn't think a Great Dane would have to be told."

"Usually he doesn't." Her brow knotted with a

frown. "I don't know why he wasn't here to meet me. I'll be right back."

She returned in less than five minutes. "He didn't come when I called." She came slowly toward him, the worried frown still on her face. "Crazy dog. He's probably out chasing rabbits again."

Sitting down across from him at the round oak table, she straightened her shoulders as if to shrug off a burden. "Sorry, I seem to be on an anxiety kick lately. I've been blaming it on Andrew. He can't talk back yet."

"Andrew?"

"My son. It's a boy. I asked the doctor for an amniocentesis; its a test that detects any genetic or other problems and spins off the fascinating information of the sex of the unborn child." She looked down at her coffee, her index finger gently rubbing the side of the cup. "After Mark died I needed more than a faceless entity to share my body. I needed to know my baby was all right, as well as a real person, a companion." She lifted her eyes to meet his gaze. "Do you understand?"

"Yes."

He said nothing else, yet she felt a warmth sweep through her unlike anything she had ever known. For a moment it seemed impossible to tear her gaze away from his. Her throat felt tight and she had difficulty breathing. She picked up her cup and cradled it in her palms. "I think you do. I guess it's not surprising. Mark was the most understanding man I've ever met. It must run in the family."

"I'm nothing like Mark." His tone was suddenly harsh. "Don't make the mistake of drawing comparisons that aren't there. We were as different as night and day." His lips twisted. "Inside as well as out."

What he said was true. Physically there was no resemblance between him and Mark. Jon Sandell was only a few inches taller than her five feet eight and Mark had been well over six feet. Mark also had had golden coloring with deep blue eyes and a smile as kind as summer rain. He was so incredibly handsome that people had stopped on the street to stare at him in bedazzlement. She had been dazzled herself at first and hadn't been able to believe it when he started to pursue her with gentle persistence.

There was nothing either gentle or golden about his cousin. Jon Sandell was dark and intense and composed of hard, sharp angles. She found her gaze drawn to the strong brown column of his throat and allowed it to wander down to catch the faintest glimpse of virile dark hair above the top button of his navy flannel shirt. The dark thatch of hair looked soft, springy, and suddenly, incredibly, she found her palms tingling as if she were actually touching it. The shocking sensation caused her to quickly jerk her gaze away. What had happened to her? For a moment she had felt a burst of sensuality stronger than any she had previously experienced. It was nothing, she told herself. Jon Sandell projected a raw sexuality that would have aroused a response in any woman. It didn't mean anything. Still, for a moment, along with the sensuality, she had felt a closeness, almost a bonding that was, in many ways, like the empathy she had known with Mark. "Well, I'm sure you're as kind as Mark or you wouldn't be making this courtesy call. I'm really grateful, Mr. Sandell."

"Jon. I've thought of you as Elizabeth for a long time." He sipped his coffee. "And I'm not kind. I'm here because I want to be." He paused. "And because I have to be."

She lifted an eyebrow. "Have?"

He nodded. His gaze was fixed on the lead glass windowpane above the sink. "I like your home. How old is it?"

"It's been in my family for over a hundred and eighty years. I love it too." She gazed around the large oak-beamed room with affection. "The cottage was a flour mill at one time. My ancestors built it and lived in two little rooms upstairs. It was renovated and expanded when small mills became a thing of the past." She lifted her coffee cup to her lips. "Mark loved the house, too, thank heavens. I don't know what I would have done if he'd wanted to move somewhere else."

"Yes, he told me he loved it. He said it was very restful to lie in bed and listen to the creak of the paddle wheel as it dipped into the stream." His gaze met her own. "I don't hear it now."

"It's turned off. It was converted to electricity awhile back, and I'm afraid the power to run it is a luxury, now that the stream has turned into a pleasant trickle. You wouldn't be able to hear it anyway. These stone walls are over a foot thick and the wheel is on the other side of the house."

"Outside your bedroom window." It was a statement, not a question.

Her eyes widened in surprise. "Mark must have written you in great detail. I wouldn't have thought he'd bother to describe the cottage so precisely."

"He didn't want to. I insisted. I wanted to know everything." His gaze flickered to her stomach. "Everything."

He couldn't mean . . . Elizabeth felt the hot color of a flush stain her cheeks, but she realized quickly how foolish she was being. Mark would never have shared the intimate details of their relationship even with his closest friend. She took another sip of coffee. "That's understandable, I suppose. We always want to know about the people who are close to those we love. What did he tell you about me?"

"Not enough." He was studying her with moody intensity. "Not nearly enough."

"Well, there wasn't much to tell," she said lightly. "I was a twenty-eight-year-old spinster with a house and a dog and three years to go on my bachelor's degree in library science, when Mark swept into my life. He came, he saw, he conquered."

"So I understand." Once again there was an inexplicable harshness in his tone. His lids lowered to partially veil his eyes, as he caught the uneasiness of her expression. "You were happy with him?"

"Oh, yes." Her eyes glowed softly. "He was the kindest, gentlest human being I've ever met. We only had six months together before the accident took his life, but they were the happiest I've ever known."

"You didn't have many men to compare him with. After all, you were practically housebound nursing your father all those years."

So Mark had told him about her father as well, she realized. "Those were happy years too. I loved my father and wanted to help him. I wasn't a victim of circumstances, I chose to live my life that way. I've never regretted the choice." A brilliant smile illuminated her face. "And then Mark came into my life, and now the baby. Isn't it wonderful that when one love is taken away we're given another to replace it?"

The hard lines of his face softened as he studied her eager expression. "Wonderful," he echoed quietly.

The odd breathless feeling returned, and her hand trembled as she set her cup down in the saucer. "I'm afraid Mark didn't tell me very much about you. I didn't even know you existed until shortly before he died, and even then he wasn't very informative."

"What did he tell you?"

She held up two fingers as she enumerated the facts she knew. "That you worked out of the country. That I would be able to trust you as much as I trusted him." She held up a third finger, her brown eyes dancing. "And that you weren't as tough as you seemed. I got the impression you were some kind of mercenary or something."

"No." He was silent for a moment. "It was generous of Mark to speak so favorably of me. I don't think I would have been as generous under the circumstances."

She frowned in puzzlement. "Generous? Why shouldn't he—"

"Never mind." He made an impatient motion with his hand. "It's not important right now. What's important is that you trust me as Mark asked you to." He paused. "I've rented a place in the mountains near Saranac Lake. I want you to pack a suitcase and come with me right now. Tonight."

Two

"What—" She broke off, her eyes widening in shock. "You have to be kidding?"

He shook his head. "I don't find the situation at all amusing. Unless you come with me, I believe you'll be even less amused." He leaned forward, the muscles of his shoulders coiled, vibrating with tension. "Come with me. Trust me. You won't be sorry."

"Just like that?" she asked blankly. "In case you haven't noticed, I'm almost nine months pregnant. In another three weeks my baby will be born. I'm not about to go on a jaunt into the mountains. I'm only twenty minutes away from a hospital here on the outskirts of Albany."

"I wouldn't let anything happen to you or your child." There was absolute certainty both in his voice and in his expression.

She believed him. She had the feeling he'd

use every ounce of his strength to keep her safe. The impression was so vivid, she had an almost irresistible impulse to yield to it. She hadn't been able to lean on anyone in a long time. "Look, I realize you want to help me." She reached out and covered his hand as it lay on the table. His body went perfectly still. Was he one of those people who disliked being touched? Well, if he was, it was just too bad. She was a very tactile person, and she found it difficult to communicate without touching. She kept her hand where it was. "You came here and saw a widow in a very delicate, awkward position, seemingly alone and vulnerable. You remembered how much you cared for Mark, and now you want to do something to make his wife's way a little easier." She met his gaze. "Perhaps you even feel guilty because you weren't here to lend me support at the funeral."

"You have it all worked out," he said, never lifting his gaze from her hand clasping his own.

"It wasn't all that difficult. I think Mark was right. You're not as tough as you look." Her hand tightened on his. "But you have to understand I'm a good deal tougher than I appear, too, and I'm *not* vulnerable or alone. I have friends, and I have my baby. I'll be fine."

"Friends who are two miles away, and a baby who hasn't arrived on the scene yet. I wouldn't say your arguments are convincing. I think you'd just better put yourself in my hands."

She automatically glanced down at the hand she was holding. They were strong hands, capable and sure, hands that would never falter. She gave his hand a final squeeze and released it. "But I can't do that. I have to take care of myself. We all have to live our own lives." She made a face. "And I can't see why you'd want to burden yourself with a woman in my condition so soon after your arrival from abroad. You must have all kind of things you want to do now that you're back in the States."

"You're wrong. There's nothing I'd rather do than care for you."

"Well, it's out of the question. So forget it."

"I can't forget it." As he lifted his lids, she was struck by the impact of brilliant dark eyes. "Because you don't know what the hell you're talking about. I don't feel guilty and it's not family loyalty that's dictating my desire to keep you safe. It's simply a necessity. You're in danger, dammit."

"Danger?" She gazed at him in disbelief. "What danger could I possibly be in?"

"Lord, now I've frightened you," he growled in profound self-disgust. "I didn't mean to come out with it so abruptly. I could shock you into labor or something."

"I'm hardly that fragile," she said dryly. "Though you did surprise me." And frightened her, she thought to herself. There had been no doubt of the seriousness of his statement. "Why should—"

"It's a little complicated to explain. Mark belonged to a group the government is investigating. They may think you belong to the same group, or at least have knowledge of them."

She felt waves of surprise roll over her. "Mark was involved with a subversive organization?

That's crazy. He would never had supported a group like that."

"It wasn't a subversive organization. He didn't belong to any group that posed a threat to the government." He paused. "But he did belong to a group under suspicion, and the NIB isn't known to wait patiently while their suspicions are checked out. The National Intelligence Bureau can be quite ruthlessly effective in their actions."

"Are you saying the NIB might have had Mark . . . killed?"

"No," he said quickly. "Mark's death was entirely natural. The NIB didn't become active in the investigation until later.'

"I don't understand any of this." She shook her head in an effort to clear it. "Mark wasn't even interested in politics. He was a professor of English on sabbatical. It doesn't make sense."

"Do you believe me?" he asked quietly.

Yes, she believed him, she realized. And that was even more incredible than what he had told her. There was no avoiding the naked sincerity in his gaze as he looked at her. "Are you sure?" she whispered.

"Yes."

She was silent for a long time, as she tried to sort reason out of chaos. "Then I believe you. But that doesn't mean I'll be in any danger. I'll just explain I know nothing about Mark's political activities."

He shook his head. "Bardot is a fanatic. He's been biding his time, but now he's ready to make his move."

"Bardot?"

"Karl Bardot, NIB."

"You appear to be very well informed." Her expression was wary. "I don't suppose it's possible that you belong to the same organization as Mark did?"

"Yes."

She had expected the answer. "Oh dear, I was afraid you were."

"Why afraid?" He frowned. "I told you there was no threat involved. Particularly not to you. All you have to do is come with me, and I'll see that you're taken care of."

"I can't do that. This is my home. I don't even know you." Her fingers ran distractedly through her nut-brown hair. "You walk in here and tell me I should leave everything that's dear and familiar to me just because—"

"Mark told you to trust me."

"Not with my baby." Her tone was suddenly fierce.

A faint smile touched his lips. "Does that mean you'd trust me if the child wasn't involved?"

"I think so." Her expression was troubled. "Oh, I don't know. I believe you mean well, but it's all so bizarre. If I'm innocent, there can't be any danger to me. This is America, for goodness' sake."

"You won't come with me?"

She shook her head. "You have to be mistaken. I'm sure I'll be fine once I've explained I don't know anything about all this.'

"I didn't think you would, but it was worth a chance." He set his cup down and pushed his chair away from the table. "You're tired and hungry. I'll leave now so that you can have your meal and get some rest."

"You're leaving?" She didn't know why she experienced a sudden panic.

"I've said what I had to say." He stood up and shrugged into his coat. "I'd like you to promise me something before I go."

"Promise?"

"I want you to promise me you won't let Bardot lure you out of the cottage on any pretext, that you won't get in a car or even go for a walk with him."

She felt a cold chill ripple through her. She smiled tremulously. "That won't be difficult. I probably won't even meet the man."

"Do you promise?"

"I promise," she whispered.

"You look like a big-eyed little girl," he said softly. "Don't worry. You're making it very difficult for me, but I won't let anything happen to you. That's what I'm here for."

She stood up, suddenly feeling a ridiculous sense of profound relief and well-being. "Are you staying in Albany?"

He shook his head. "I'll be around." He fastened the buttons of his jacket. "I can find my own way out. Don't see me to the door, it's too cold outside. The weather report said we should expect snow tomorrow night. That might be interesting."

Snow, interesting? What a curious turn of phrase. "You're obviously not from upstate New York or you wouldn't find the possibility of a November snowstorm very interesting." Her expression became wistful. "I'll be sorry to see the first snow. I love the summer. I spend most of my time outdoors from April until September." She suddenly grimaced. "I guess you can tell. I'm positively covered with freckles."

"Yes, I can tell." He turned away. "Goodbye, Beth, I'll see you soon."

"Beth?" She raised an eyebrow inquiringly. "My name is Elizabeth. No one calls me Beth.'

"Not even Mark?"

"No."

There was a flicker of satisfaction on his face. "Goodbye, Beth."

Not waiting for a reply, he turned and left the kitchen. A moment later she heard the front door close.

She stood there for a while, her mind a wild jumble of tattered impressions and half-formed thoughts. Jon Sandell had been there less than an hour, she realized, but he had managed to throw her into a state of complete confusion. Her heart was pounding, and her skin was tingling as if she'd just been through a Finnish sauna. Fear. Yes, fear and something else which was not so easily defined. Suddenly she was jolted out of her confusion by the most basic action possible: Andrew kicked her with force and precision.

Her hand went to her abdomen. "All right, I can take a hint. I should think good thoughts and eat dinner. Right, kid?" She turned briskly and walked toward the counter where the Crockpot still bubbled. "Nag, nag, nag."

She didn't have much hope for good thoughts,

but she did feel better after she'd had a bowl of stew and another half-cup of coffee. She gazed wistfully out the window as the tap water filled the sink, and she prepared to wash the dishes. It was entirely dark outside, and she could no longer see the narrow ribbon of the stream or the woods that lay beyond the meadow.

"'You'll have to get a blanket so I can lay him down."

She whirled with a startled little cry. Jon Sandell stood in the doorway of the kitchen. In his arms was a mass of lean, tawny fur and . . . blood.

"Sam?" She could barely speak. "Oh, no!"

"He's not hurt badly. You should take him to the vet tomorrow to have a preventive shot, but after you clean the wound he should be fine. The blanket," he prompted.

"What?" she murmured in distraction, her gaze still fixed agonizingly on Sam. "Oh, yes, right away." She moved at an amazingly fast pace from the room to the bathroom closet and grabbed the first blanket she could find from the shelf. In an instant she was back in the kitchen, doubling the blanket and spreading it on the hearth. "You're sure he's not badly hurt?" she asked anxiously. "There's a vet just—"

"He's fine." Jon knelt and put the dog down carefully on the blanket. His big hands were gentle as he arranged Sam's legs and settled his weight more evenly. The animal gave a low whimper, and Jon immediately stroked his long sleek nose. "Easy. You're home now, boy."

Elizabeth could feel hot tears stinging her eyes. "What happened to him?"

Jon pointed to the ugly red gash that extended in a straight line from behind Sam's front paw to the middle of his back. "Bullet. It only grazed him, but he's not going to feel like chasing rabbits for a while."

Elizabeth could feel the blood leave her face. "A hunter?" She moistened her lips with her tongue. "It must have been a hunter who mistook Sam for a deer."

"Perhaps." He gave Sam a final pat and rose to his feet. "Would you like me to stay, or can you manage by yourself?"

"I can manage. Where did you find him? On the road?"

"In the woods."

She turned in surprise to face him. "What were you doing in the woods?"

"I was searching for your Heinz 57. I knew as soon as you had time to think about him that you'd be out looking for him yourself. I didn't want you stumbling around in the dark." He met her gaze. "Was I wrong?"

"No," she whispered. "Thank you, Jon."

He smiled with surprising gentleness. "He's a brave dog. I like your Sam, Beth." He turned away. "Take good care of him."

"I will."

The door had scarcely closed behind him when she was kneeling beside the dog, cleaning the wound with soap and water. Jon was right. Though the wound was shallow it had to be very painful for poor Sam. Yet the dog was mutely patient, and he gave only an occasional whimper as the antibiotic cream Elizabeth applied stung the wound.

"You *are* a good dog, aren't you, boy," she murmured. "He likes you. Do you know that? And that provides him with some pretty heavy credentials for good taste in this household. As for the rest, he's still a bit of a mystery. I guess we'll just have to wait and see."

The night was clear and frigid, and each breath Jon drew released a wisp of smoky vapor into the air. He opened the door of the pickup, stepped up into the cab, and slammed the door. He sat for a moment gazing at the lights gleaming from the windows of the cottage. Elizabeth in the firelight. The memory lingered with an aching sharpness, reaching deep into his mind and triggering responses better left unexamined. He finally tore his gaze away and reached for the mobile phone beneath the dashboard.

Gunner Nilsen answered on the second ring. "Yes?"

"I've made contact."

"And?"

"She refused to leave the cottage."

"Well, you expected as much. You told me yourself it wasn't likely you could persuade her to trust you that far."

"No, but I had to try." There was weariness threading his voice. "She's with child, dammit. I wanted to make it as easy as I could for her."

"I know, Jon."

"How is it up there?"

"The lodge is comfortable and the location exactly what you wanted."

"You covered your tracks?"

Gunner chuckled. "I not only covered them, I buried them. As far as the leasing agency is concerned, the lodge is being rented by a Wall Street tycoon for his snow-bunny mistress. Did you hear it was going to snow tomorrow? I'm looking forward to it. I bought skis from the sports shop in town."

"Wonderful," Jon said ironically. "All we need is for you to break your leg on one of the slopes."

"It can't be that much different from sand skiing," Gunner protested. "I'll be careful." There was a short pause. "Is she the person you expected?"

Jon turned the question over in his mind. He had a sudden vivid picture of Elizabeth Ramsey as he'd last seen her. She'd been standing in the kitchen, her body seemingly too fragile to support the burden of the child she was carrying, her straight brown hair shining richly in the firelight, the sleeves of her loose blue shirt rolled up to reveal strong, shapely arms. She had said herself that she wasn't pretty, and perhaps she wasn't by classic standards. The slightly upward tilt of her nose and the golden freckles dusting her face weren't conventionally attractive.

Freckles touched by the summer sun she loved. She was the kind of woman anyone would want to touch, to leave a sign of affection upon in passing so she would remember . . . and smile. Lord, he loved her smile. He had expected it, had known how warm and lovely it would be, but he had still found himself staring at her like a gaping boy. He'd found himself glancing away quickly in order to resist the impulse to reach out and trace the source of that smile with his finger.

Mark had probably done that. Jon felt a hot surge of possessive rage at the thought. Mark had touched her breasts, stroked her hair. He had thrust into her body and . . . Jon drew a deep breath and tried to block out the thought. He mustn't think of Mark and Elizabeth together. He had to forget those images. He had to keep the savagely possessive aspect of his nature under control. Mark was a part of her past. Elizabeth was his now. She didn't know it yet, but she would soon. All the glowing warmth and gentle humor that was Elizabeth would belong to him.

"Jon?"

He forced his hand to relax on the receiver of the mobile phone as he quickly collected his thoughts and answered Gunner's question. "More. She's much more, Gunner."

"That's good." Gunner's voice was gentle. "I'm happy for you. When will you be arriving here?"

"By tomorrow night, I hope. Bardot's showing signs of impatience. I think he'll approach her directly and try to use the element of surprise to get the information from her. If the bastard acts with his usual charm and tact, he'll probably scare her into jumping in our direction."

"What if you're wrong? What if he brings help and forces her to go with him to the farm?"

"I don't think we have to worry. Bardot's superiors are already doubting his credibility. He'll want proof if he can get it." His voice roughened. "And if I'm wrong, you can forget all that bilge they gave us about nonviolence and a low profile. I won't let Bardot take her."

"They put you in charge. No one is going to say anything if you find it necessary to change tactics."

"They'd better not. I've run out of patience too. The cost has been too high already." Jon's gaze returned to the cottage. "I'll let you know if we have to switch gears."

"Do that. I can't say I've liked this waiting game we've been playing any more than you have. I could use a little action."

"You speak as if action's an unusual state," Jon said dryly. "I've never known a time when you haven't preferred trouble to the serene life."

"It's a quality you've always found useful in the past," Gunner drawled. "If I remember correctly, you're the one who saved my neck when those guards in Said Ababa decided to separate it from my magnificent body." He paused. "Be careful, Jon. If you have to go on the offensive, make it clean."

Jon didn't need Gunner to warn him of the consequences of leaving loose ends on this project. "I'm neither a novice nor a fool, Gunner. I'll see you tomorrow." He hung up the receiver and started the motor and then backed out of the driveway.

He drove only a short distance down the road before turning off into the woods and positioning the truck to get a clear view of the cottage. He switched off the ignition and the lights, and leaned back in the seat. It was going to be a cold night, much colder than the previous ones he'd spent sitting there guarding Elizabeth and her unborn child. He turned up the collar of his coat and concentrated for a moment, blocking the cold from his consciousness. Even in the protection of the cab he could see his breath mist before him.

He had to think, to plan his next move in case he was wrong about the way Bardot was going to react. He was grateful to have something to think about during the long night ahead. It would distract him from remembering the image of Elizabeth touched by firelight. God knows, he'd need that distraction.

Three

"Mrs. Ramsey, my name is Karl Bardot, I'm with the National Intelligence Bureau. I have to speak with you." The large man standing on the steps was staring at her with belligerence, as he flicked open his wallet to show his I.D. "May I come in?"

Bardot. A tiny tingle of fear ran through her. She had been telling herself Jon Sandell was mistaken, that she would never be confronted by Bardot. But just because he was now here there was no reason to assume he was a threat to her, she assured herself quickly.

She stepped aside. "Come in, please, Mr. Bardot." She turned and preceded him across the hall and through the arched opening to the sitting room. "I've just made some coffee. Would you like a cup?"

He shook his head. "This isn't a social call. I have a few questions to ask you." He was gazing at her with cold dislike. "How you answer my questions will determine whether it's necessary to take you into custody."

"Arrest me?" He couldn't be serious. "That's absurd. I haven't done anything wrong."

"Not yet maybe, but I said I could take you into custody, not arrest you. Sometimes it's necessary to remove the source of an infestation before national security is actually endangered."

The scene was playing like a Grade B movie, Elizabeth thought. Bardot was definitely a Grade B villain she decided, with his heavy jowls, thinning gray hair and pale blue eyes. "I don't know what you're talking about." She met his gaze calmly. "But I do know my rights as an American citizen. Without a specific charge you can't touch me. That's the law, Mr. Bardot."

"Can't I?" His lips twisted unpleasantly. "You're a bit out of touch with reality, Mrs. Ramsey." He glanced around the room appraisingly. "This is quite a place. All of these eighteenth-century antiques must be worth a bundle."

"This is my home. I'd never think of putting a price tag on any of my possessions."

"No, I guess not. You've never had to worry about money. Your father left you a tidy little sum in insurance money when he died, didn't he?" He didn't wait for an answer. "And I'm sure your husband set you up so you'd be safe and sound as far as funds are concerned. Money can buy a hell of a lot of protection."

"My husband left me nothing. He was a professor of English at the University of Michigan." She tried to keep the anger from her tone. Answer his

questions and get him out of here, she had thought
initially, but it was becoming increasingly difficult. "Teachers don't make a lot of money, you
know."

"The University of Michigan never heard of Mark
Ramsey," Bardot said. "Oh, someone took the trouble of planting a dossier in their computer to
substantiate his story in case it was checked. But
an on-the-spot investigation revealed that he never
set foot on the campus." His cold gaze raked over
her face. "You appear shocked. You were married
to the man. You must have been privy to his
secrets."

"No!" Her head was whirling and she felt sick.
Mark had lied to her. Why? He must have known
there could be nothing in his past that would
alter the way she felt about him. Well, whatever
the subterfuge, it must have been for a good reason. Mark never would have done anything wrong.
"There must be some misunderstanding. Mark
was no criminal."

"You're a very good actress. Ramsey chose well."
Bardot paused and then asked sharply, "Where
were you earlier today? I came by and you weren't
at home. You don't have classes on Friday."

"How did you know—" She broke off. Of course
he'd know. If he'd been thorough enough to find
out Mark hadn't taught at the university, his investigation of her must have been just as pains-
taking. "I took my dog to the vet."

"Your dog?" A flicker of surprise crossed his
face.

She nodded absently. "This is ridiculous, I know

nothing about any plots that might endanger security, and neither did Mark."

"You know. You think you've bamboozled us. You *have* fooled some of the idiots upstairs. They think I'm crazy to believe the intelligence reports from Said Ababa." His pale blue eyes were burning with a fanatical passion. "But you haven't fooled me. I know what you are and I'm going to stop you."

She stared at him in disbelief. "Your superiors are right. You are crazy. There's absolutely nothing to stop. Mark may have lied about his background, but he couldn't have been guilty of any wrongdoing." Her voice was trembling and she tried to still it. "You don't understand. Mark was very special."

His laugh was more of a mirthless bark. "Very amusing. I'm aware of how 'special' your husband was. I have a report in my files that verifies several aspects of his uniqueness."

She shook her head in bewilderment. "I don't understand."

"You understand all right," he said. "You'd be wise to avoid annoying me by playing stupid. I've waited a long time, and I'm getting impatient. If you're not going to cooperate, then I think I'd better take you to our headquarters for interrogation. Go pack a suitcase."

It was the second time in twenty-four hours that she'd been asked to pack a suitcase, she thought wildly. Only this time it was hardly an invitation. "It sounds like you plan on having me stay awhile." Promise me you won't go with him, Sandell had said. She couldn't think straight. A government man couldn't be a threat to her. She was a citizen with rights and privileges. Yet she had heard stories . . .

Her hand moved with instinctive protectiveness to her abdomen. "No! I won't go with you. My child is due soon and I won't let this insanity threaten him. There are laws in this country protecting citizens."

"Which can be suspended in wartime."

"We're not at war." She realized her words were making no impression on the man. He was gazing at her with . . . Lord, the emotion couldn't be hatred. He didn't even know her. Yet, if it wasn't hatred, it was close enough to fill her with terror. Hatred led to violence and she couldn't run the risk of exposing her son to violence. They were both too vulnerable now. "I think you'd better leave."

"I can force you to go."

"You could try." She met his gaze. "But I'd fight you and I think you should know I have a dog in the kitchen who can be very protective. A very large dog."

Uneasiness flickered in Bardot's face as he glanced around furtively. He turned to the door. "I'll be back. If I were you, I wouldn't leave the area. You'll find the roads are being watched."

The gray Ford sedan. She shivered and folded her arms across her chest. "Harassment is illegal. I'm going to phone my attorney."

The glance he shot her was one of acid mixed with malice. "You're up to all the tricks, aren't you? I'm surprised you slipped up and signed your husband's autopsy authorization after his automobile accident. Did you think you were safe with a small-town coroner? He was sharper than you gave him credit for."

Elizabeth could feel the blood draining from her face. "Are you accusing me of murder?"

"You know what I'm accusing you of. It was very clever having him cremated."

"Clever! He left a letter requesting his body be cremated. I was just obeying his wishes."

"Very convenient." He smiled crookedly. "Goodbye, Mrs. Ramsey. I'd pack that suitcase if I were you. My men might not choose what you'd like to wear when I come back." A few seconds later the front door closed behind him.

Elizabeth stood motionless, feeling as if she had been hit by a truck. Bardot had meant every word he had said. His malevolence had been too clear to mistake. Why?

Sam was yelping and jumping against the kitchen door, and Elizabeth moved dazedly from the sitting room down the carpeted hall to the kitchen. What could she do? She couldn't allow herself to be placed in Bardot's hands, and she had heard too many stories of federal agencies and local law enforcement officials working hand and glove, to trust the local police for protection.

Sam's yelps grew wilder and more savage, almost frantic, as she drew near. He was throwing himself against the door as if he were trying to knock it down.

She opened the door. "Sam, are you trying to hurt yourself? Stop—" She broke off as the dog catapulted through the opening, knocking her against the wall. He tore down the hall and leaped against the Dutch door, growling savagely.

"Sam, what's gotten into you?" Then the significance of the dog's actions became clear to her. Bardot. She remembered the surprise on his face when she had mentioned taking Sam to the vet. He was surprised because he thought he had killed Sam the night before! she realized. "Oh, no." She sank down on the third step of the staircase, feeling sick. She stared dumbly at the dog, still hurling himself at the door trying to get at the man who had left him for dead in the woods. So much violence. How could her life have changed so radically in less than twenty-four hours?

An authoritative rat-a-tat sounded at the door. "Beth, let me in. We don't have much time."

"Jon!"

Jumping up from the step, she ran the few feet to the front door, pushed Sam aside, and fumbled with the lock. "Jon, he was here. That Bardot man . . ." She threw open the door. Sam bolted past her only to be caught by Jon before he could leave the steps.

"Call him. We don't have time to chase him down," Jon said tersely.

"Come, Sam. *Now!*"

Sam gave a last protesting growl and trotted back into the foyer.

Jon followed him into the cottage and closed the door.

"Bardot was here. He said crazy things. He's a terrible man." The words were tumbling from Elizabeth's lips. Her eyes were wide and stricken as she gazed up at him. "I think he shot Sam."

"I suspected he did." He stepped closer and pulled her into his arms. Warmth, safety, the scent of soap and musk. "Shh, it's going to be all right. I won't let him hurt you. No one will ever hurt you again."

Her arms slid around his waist to clutch him desperately. The wool of his mackinaw was rough against her cheek. "He was going to take me somewhere. I told him I couldn't go, but he wouldn't listen. He thinks I killed Mark."

"Killed?" His tone was puzzled. "He said that?"

"He implied it. At least I think he did. Oh, I don't know. It was something about the autopsy and cremation." She lifted her head, her eyes misting with tears. "He *hates* me, Jon. I don't think anyone has ever hated me before. It frightened me. My baby—"

"—will be fine," Jon finished with great firmness.

"He's coming back. He said he was coming back with some of his men."

"We'll be gone by then. It'll take an hour for him to get to the farm and back. By that time, we'll be a quarter of the way to the lodge."

"Farm?"

"Bardot's agency has a charming compound not far from here known as the farm. It's completely isolated." His lips twisted into a grim frown. "Isolation can be very convenient when interrogating prisoners."

"Was that where he was going to take me?"

"Yes, but I wouldn't have let him." His arms released her and his hands moved up to cradle her face. He looked into her eyes. "Will you go with me now?"

"I don't understand any of this. I know Mark is innocent but— "

"I realize you could never doubt a paragon like Mark." His lips tightened. "I'll make no pretense of having any of his sterling qualities. You'll have to accept me as I am. However, I think you'll find I can keep you safe."

The antagonism in his voice made her uneasy and she made a motion to brush his hands away from her face.

"No," he said fiercely. "Don't flinch away from me. I may not be Mark but I . . ." His breath released explosively. "I'm not being very persuasive, am I?"

She shook her head. "Tell me what this is all about and I'll come with you."

"I can't do that. Not right now. I hope I'll be able to tell you everything soon. Is that good enough?"

"I don't have much choice. It's either you or Bardot." Her eyes were suddenly blazing up at him. "I don't like this, Jon. I don't like being frightened out of my home or used as a pawn in a game I don't understand. And I particularly don't like my life disrupted, and my child's welfare threatened. I'll go with you, because right now it appears to be best. And I've already made arrangements with my professors to complete my courses at home after the baby comes. But you wait until my baby is born and safe from all this madness, and I'll show you and Bardot I'm not to be manipulated."

She didn't know what his response to her statement would be, but she didn't expect the mixture of pride and amusement she saw in his expression. "I'll be looking forward to it." His fingers brushed her cheek in a light caress before he stepped back. "Go turn off the gas and electricity while I put Sam in the truck. Will your friend, Serena, take care of him until we can reclaim him?"

Elizabeth nodded. "Do I have time to pack?"

"Just grab a warm coat and gloves. We'll find you something to wear at the lodge." He stooped and picked up the dog. A moment before Sam had been fiercely aggressive, but now he appeared amazingly docile in Jon's arms.

The man must be incredibly strong, she thought absently as she opened the door for him. He was carrying Sam with easy strength and the dog weighed over a hundred pounds. "Bardot said the road would be watched."

"It *was* watched," Jon said over his shoulder. "It's not now. I took care of Bardot's man when I saw Bardot pull up at the cottage."

"Took care of?" Elizabeth asked, startled.

"Eliminated." His lips twisted. "Not permanently. I may have violent instincts, but I don't always indulge them. Hurry, we have to get moving."

"My God, he's going to kill himself!" Elizabeth stared in horror as a skier hurtled down the steep slope of a nearby mountain, heading toward their truck as they drove along the road. Dressed in a scarlet-colored ski suit that made his white-blond hair appear even more brilliant in contrast, the man had all the grace of a pregnant hippopotamus as he leaned precariously from side to side, trying to maintain his balance. "He must be a novice. Why would he risk a run on a dangerous slope like that?"

"Because he's a reckless idiot who can't resist—" Jon broke off as he pulled the pickup to the side of the road and turned off the ignition. "Stay here." He jumped out of the cab onto the road, cupped his hands around his mouth and shouted with a force that echoed through the mountains. "Gunner, blast you. I told you to be careful. What the hell do you think you're doing? Trying to break your damn neck?"

The blond skier shouted back, laughing. "I'm doing very well, Jon. It's a little more difficult than sand and harder when you fall, but give me a week and I'll be a world-class expert."

"Give you a week, and you'll be in a plaster cast from your collarbone to your toes," Jon said grimly.

The skier was drawing nearer to the road, still, by some miracle, in an upright position. "Is that kind? Just ask me again to go to the trouble of coming to welcome you to our happy home." He chuckled. "I'd turn around and ski off in a huff except for one thing."

"What's that?"

"I don't know how to turn." His deep laugh boomed in the tranquil surroundings. "So I'll be magnanimous and forgive you under the circumstances. Particularly since I'll have to beg for a ride back to the lodge."

"Do you know how to stop?"

"Oh, sure, I learned that in the first five minutes. Watch."

Suddenly he threw himself backward into the

snow, his skis pointing to the sky. The momentum twisted his body in a corkscrew before flopping him face forward into a snowbank.

Was he hurt? He wasn't moving. Only a moment before the blond skier had been so vibrantly alive and now . . . Elizabeth fumbled for the door handle and then jumped out on the hard-packed snow. She half ran, half slid around the truck and across the road. Jon was several yards ahead of her, climbing the slope with swift powerful strides.

He was kneeling beside the scarlet-clad figure and was carefully turning him over as she reached them.

"Gunner, are you crazy?" Jon's voice was husky despite its roughness. "Why don't you ever do what I tell you? Where does it hurt?"

"Do you mean where besides my pride?" The skier's lids opened to reveal deep blue eyes that were dancing with mischief. "Well, I'll probably have to sit on a pillow for a week or two, but other than that I've probably come off lucky."

"As usual." Beneath the gruffness of Jon's tone, it was clear to Elizabeth he was greatly relieved. Affection and lingering anxiety were only lightly veiled by the half-mocking sarcasm in his tone. "I don't know why I'm surprised. You wouldn't be here today if the gods didn't love you. Are you sure you haven't broken anything?"

"I'm sure." The skier sat up and began unbuckling his right ski. "You know, Jon, I think I'll try to find another way to stop. This method is a little rough on the . . ." He trailed off as his gaze encountered Elizabeth's over Jon's shoulder.

"Hello. You must be Elizabeth Ramsey. I'm Gunner Nilsen."

Jon turned to her, frowning. "I thought I told you to stay in the truck."

"You did," Elizabeth said calmly. "I didn't choose to obey you. You'll find I seldom do what I'm ordered to do. It's far more effective to ask me politely."

Gunner Nilsen uttered a sound that was not a cough and not a chortle. Jon cast him a scowling glance, and Gunner threw up his hands in surrender. "Sorry. I was just thinking how long it's been since anyone has put you down so nicely. As I remember it was the head of the committee for—"

"Gunner." Jon's voice cut through his words with the crisp incisiveness of a machete. "The fall must have rattled what little brains you have. It's certainly loosened your tongue."

"Sorry," Gunner said again, unrepentantly. He finished unfastening his left ski and slid both of them off his feet. "I suppose I felt safe. I forgot she doesn't know yet."

Know what? Elizabeth thought in exasperation. This situation was progressing from frustration to complete madness. "Yet? I presume I'm supposed to have this great mystery revealed soon?"

"That's up to Jon." Gunner rose lightly to his feet and smiled beguilingly at her. "I'm just a poor peon under orders."

The "poor peon" smiling at her had all the charm of a gypsy horse trader and the stunning good looks of a male model. He was taller than Jon by at least two inches and had the same deeply bronzed complexion. He was a golden man with the same aura of glamour Mark had possessed. But Mark's good looks had never possessed Gunner's blatant sexuality and joie de vivre. Mark's appeal had been gentle and deep and wise as . . . She glanced away hurriedly. "You bear more resemblance to Mark than Jon does. Are you another cousin?"

Jon looked up swiftly. "He reminds you of Mark?"

"A little."

Gunner's sideways glance at Jon was both amused and wary. "I wouldn't presume to admit to such august company. The committee said I must have the genes of a highwayman."

Elizabeth frowned in puzzlement. "What?"

"Gunner." This time Jon's tone was definitely menacing.

"Oh, all right." Gunner scooped up his skis and balanced them against his left shoulder. "I guess if I don't keep my mouth shut I'll be trekking back to the lodge through the snow instead of riding in luxurious splendor in the back of the pickup. Right?"

"Right," Jon said as he rose to his feet and turned away. His hand was cupping Elizabeth's elbow as he helped her carefully down the slope.

Gunner passed them at a trot, skidding and sliding down to the road with careless disregard. He threw his skis into the bed of the pickup and then hoisted his tall, lean body after them.

Jon's gaze moodily followed Gunner's movements. "I don't see any likeness."

"What?" For a moment she didn't know to what he was referring. She had thought the subject of

Gunner's resemblance to Mark was closed. "Oh, you don't? Perhaps it's not noticeable unless you're looking for it. However, those exceptional good looks and golden coloring aren't exactly common."

"No?" He was silent a moment, scowling. "You prefer fair men?"

"I never thought about it." She shrugged. "I guess I do. I fell in love with Mark."

His lips thinned. "Yes, you fell in love with dear cousin Mark." He opened the passenger door of the truck and lifted her into the seat. "Lord, he had it easy." He slammed the car door.

Elizabeth felt a pang of hurt. Why should she care if he thought her cheap? She stared straight ahead through the windshield as he climbed into the driver's seat and started the car. She blinked rapidly to keep back the tears. "Yes, he did," she said, not looking at him. "I was totally in love with Mark. If he had told me to join the circus and become a lion tamer, I would probably have only asked which one. If that's being easy, then I guess I'm a prime example."

"I didn't mean you were . . ." His hands tightened so hard on the steering wheel his knuckles turned white. "I always thought I was fairly articulate, but I find I'm tongue-tied as a child around you. I hurt you, didn't I?"

Her voice was low and slightly uneven. "Yes."

Jon muttered a soft, vehement curse as he turned to face her. "I'm not always this rough or insensitive." His eyes, dark with intensity and pain, were gazing into her own with mesmerizing urgency, as if he would force understanding on her by sheer will alone. "There are things about this situation I can't explain, and they're hanging about my neck like an albatross. Sometimes I feel as if that damn albatross is strangling me. It rubs me raw and makes me clumsy and—" He broke off. "All those excuses don't really matter. What does matter is that you know I would never think of you with anything but respect and . . . affection." He drew a deep breath, as if he'd just reached the summit of a mountain after a hard climb. "All right?"

Suddenly she felt deflated. She should be feeling comforted and reassured, not this depressed. She smiled determinedly. "Thank you. You're very kind."

Jon turned away, his movements jerky and uncoordinated as he maneuvered the truck back onto the road. Kind. Lord, she thought he was kind. It was what he'd wanted her to think, but it still grated unbearably on his nerves. He wasn't in the least bit kind, any more than the emotions coursing through him were platonic. He wanted to touch her, draw her close so he could breathe the scent of her as he had that moment at the cottage. He wanted to take off her clothes and run his hands over the fruitful earthiness of her body. He could feel the painful tightening of his muscles and tried desperately to relax.

He hadn't expected to want her like this. Hell, she was heavy with child. He had thought he'd feel only tenderness and possessiveness. Desire had taken him by surprise. He knew he'd have to watch every word, every expression, while he was with her now. She had to be made to feel safe and cosseted during this period, and he knew the situation didn't lend itself to those emotions. All she needed was to learn she was occupying a secluded house with a man who was aching to drag her into bed and teach her erotic games of which she'd never dreamed. A man aching to wipe Mark Ramsey from her mind and body and imprint himself indelibly on both.

Wait. He wasn't an animal. He could be as patient and gentle as her precious Mark. He could forget hunger and lust and give her only what she needed from him. In a hundred ways he was stronger than Mark. The very drives he possessed that had been judged too aggressive were in his favor now. She would belong to him. If only he could forget the throbbing ache in his groin and . . .

"This area is very isolated, isn't it?" Elizabeth asked, trying to make conversation. The silence between them was charged with a disturbing electricity. "It seems impossible we're close to a popular ski resort like Saranac Lake. Do you think Bardot will be able to locate us?"

"Not for a few weeks, and by that time we won't need the place any longer."

She shot him an anxious glance. "I can't stay here in the mountains for a few weeks. I have to be near a hospital. You don't know what the winters can be like in this area. We could be snowed in for days if the storm they're predicting turns into a blizzard."

"I told you that your baby would be safe."

"I know, but . . ." Elizabeth looked out the window at the white slopes glittering against the slate-gray of the gathering clouds. There was no use worrying about problems that might never occur. She still had time and, for some reason, she had a strong faith in Jon's ability to assure her son's survival. She suddenly chuckled. "Well, I hope you have a book on midwifery at the lodge. It might come in handy."

"You'll find the library as well stocked as the cupboards. The lodge is very comfortable. A fireplace in every room, and it has its own power generator. There's no telephone or television but we have a short-wave radio in case of emergencies."

"That's a relief," Elizabeth said. "Though I hope we won't have to use it."

"I thought you'd feel better knowing we had some method of communicating with the outside world." He nodded to the left. "The lodge is up ahead."

The redwood chalet was larger than she had thought it would be. A two-story ultramodern structure composed of more glass than redwood. The interior was modern as well, she discovered a few minutes later. Bright-colored rugs covered gleaming parquet floors. The contemporary furniture was upholsterd with fabric in tones of warm brown and beige, and the abstract paintings she glimpsed were cheerful splashes of color against the pine-paneled walls of the foyer.

"I hope you like yellow," Gunner said as he preceded them up the carpeted stairs to the second floor. "Whoever decorated your room appeared to be overly fond of the color. Yellow drapes, yellow bedspread, yellow chair. The master bedroom looks like a daffodil in full bloom, but I thought you'd be more comfortable there than in one of the smaller bedrooms. At least the carpet is a nice calm beige." He threw open the second door at the head of the stairs and strolled into a large, airy room. "The master bath has both a shower stall and a tub. By the way, I installed those safety bars in the shower yesterday, Jon."

"Good." Jon stood in the doorway, his gaze on Elizabeth as she followed Gunner into the bedroom. She looked tired and rumpled and . . . wonderful. He had a sudden impulse to pick her up, hold her, cradle her. He forced himself to look away from her to the floor-to-ceiling windows occupying the entire north wall. Tenderness at last. Poignant, intense tenderness. It was going to be all right. If he could only hold on to the tenderness, it would dilute the hunger.

"I think you'll find everything you need." Gunner slid back the doors of the walk-in closet to reveal a multitude of clothing of every description. "Last week I found a very cooperative sales lady in one of the local shops, who assured me this is a maternity wardrobe par excellence."

Elizabeth had an idea there would always be cooperative ladies at Gunner's beck and call. A tiny smile curved her lips as she crossed the room to stand beside him in front of the clothing. "I'm sure she was delighted to accommodate you, but you went a little overboard. I'd have trouble wearing all these clothes in two months, and I only have three weeks."

The smile suddenly faded from her face. He said he had purchased all these clothes last week. She had not known either of these men existed a week ago and yet they had already been making plans that involved her, she realized. Buying clothes, installing safety bars, watching her cottage.

"What size are they?" she asked numbly.

"Eight," Jon said. Gunner gestured to the shoe rack on the floor. "And size seven shoes. Right?"

"Right." She couldn't take her eyes off the pink cable-knit sweater on the hanger directly in front of her. Panic was swirling through her and her heart was pounding so hard she thought it would burst through her breast. Andrew moved uneasily, jerking her to her senses. She mustn't get upset, she told herself, just breathe deeply.

"Beth." Jon was standing quietly beside her, his gaze fixed warily on her face. "What's wrong?"

She laughed shakily. "Nothing at all. What could possibly be wrong? I'm involved with ruthless government agents, and I have an idea you two could be just as ruthless. I'm drowning in intrigue and secrets, and I don't understand a damn thing."

"You'll understand everything soon. I promise."

"You've said that before." She whirled to face him. "When?"

He hesitated. "After the child is born. Does that satisfy you?"

"No, it doesn't, but it will have to do. I'll be darned if I'll let myself suffer a case of nerves that might endanger my son." She riffled through the clothes until she found a loose velour caftan in a soft rose shade and pulled it from the hanger. "Now, if you'll excuse me, I need to shower and change." She moved swiftly toward the door Gunner had indicated. "I'll be downstairs in thirty minutes, and Andrew and I would appreciate something to eat."

As the door closed firmly behind her Gunner looked inquiringly at Jon. "Andrew?"

"The baby."

"Oh." Gunner's thoughtful gaze returned to the door. "She's taking all this very well considering the circumstances. She's very strong."

"Stronger than she knows," Jon said. "Her life hasn't been easy, but she's never really been tested." He turned wearily toward the door. "She will be soon."

Four

"May I help?"

Gunner smiled as he looked up from the onions he was sautéing at the stove. "Don't you dare. There's a certain slapdash pizzazz to the art of cooking that suits my temperament admirably. I enjoy the hell out of it." His deep blue eyes studied her critically. "You look more relaxed. The shower must have done you a lot of good."

She wrinkled her nose at him. "You mean besides making me more socially acceptable? It did help. I love the feel of warm water pouring over me. Where's Jon?"

"Outside on the deck." His gaze returned to the frying pan. "Dinner will be ready in about twenty minutes. I hope Andrew likes steak and onions."

"We're both crazy about them. Are you sure I can't do anything?"

Gunner shook his head. "Go into the living room

and put your feet up in front of the fire. I want you nice and serene when Jon sees you next. He ripped me apart verbally for my unorthodox appearance on the scene. He thought I frightened you."

"You did. I was sure you were going to break your neck."

"There was the slightest possibility I wasn't in complete control," he admitted with a grin. "Next time I'll do better. I didn't mean to worry you. I had this vision of flying down the mountain like an eagle and impressing you with my daring."

"Well, you certainly succeeded," she said, smiling. "Though I don't know why you would go to the trouble."

"Why shouldn't I want to impress you? You're Jon's lady and he—" He broke off and was silent for a moment, avoiding her shocked gaze. "I have an idea I'm in for another tongue-lashing from my honorable commandant. Forget I said that, will you?"

"I'm not Jon Sandell's . . . lady. You must have misunderstood something he said," she said haltingly. "I was married to his cousin, Mark."

He glanced up, and a brilliant smile lit up his tanned face. "You're right. I probably misunderstood. Now, run along and rest."

He was trying to distract her and make her forget his incredible verbal slip. Elizabeth was sure that behind Gunner's boisterous, careless charm lay a man who made very few mistakes. However, the alternative was that Jon Sandell had indicated he thought of her in terms of . . . She couldn't complete the thought, as hot color flushed her cheeks and stung through her veins. It couldn't be true. He was Mark's cousin, for goodness' sake. Yet there had been a thread of puzzling antagonism in his manner when he spoke of Mark, and a queer electric awareness sparked between them since the moment he had come down the steps of the cottage yesterday afternoon. The way she had tingled when she had looked at him in the kitchen . . . No! If she had experienced any sexual attraction, it must have been a reflection of what Jon Sandell was feeling. Oh, Lord, that didn't make sense either. In her present condition, her sex appeal was non-existent. "I believe it's time I had a discussion with Jon. You say he's on the deck?"

He nodded gloomily. "I was afraid you wouldn't let it pass. I guess I'd better hold dinner for another thirty minutes."

"It might be wise."

"My jacket is in the hall closet. Put it on before you go outside. I'm going to be in enough trouble without letting you stalk out there and risk pneumonia."

"I don't stalk. It's much too melodramatic, and I'm very careful about running any risk at all these days. I particularly refuse to risk mental stress when I can probably straighten out the situation with a few minutes of conversation." She smiled fleetingly. "Andrew doesn't like me to be upset."

"Neither does Jon. Which means I'm due to catch hell. Tell them both I'm profoundly sorry." He sighed. "That's certainly bloody well true."

A smile was still lingering on Elizabeth's lips as she slipped Gunner's warm suede coat on over her caftan. Her smile vanished, however, when she opened the front door and caught sight of Jon standing with his back to her staring out into the darkness. A light snow was beginning to fall, and a few glittering flakes were captured in the sable darkness of his hair. For the first time since she had met him, he looked totally relaxed. "Jon."

He whirled toward her, an expression of wariness on his face that hurt her in the same strange way his careless words had earlier in the truck. He was so terribly guarded, every movement charged with painful intensity. She had a sudden desire to soothe away the wariness, hold him until he felt safe and . . . Good Lord, what was she thinking? Jon Sandell needed protection less than any man she'd ever met. She closed the door behind her. "I want to talk to you."

He relaxed. "Fine. We'd better go inside, it's too cold out here for you."

"No. This will only take a moment. I need the fresh air." And the darkness. The question she had to ask him was embarrassing enough without having to face his keen dark eyes. She crossed to stand beside him. "The snow isn't falling very fast, is it? Maybe the Weather Bureau was wrong about the storm."

"Perhaps."

She could feel his gaze on her face, and her hands closed tightly on the rough wood of the railing. "I know what I'm going to ask you is silly. It's all probably some idiotic misunderstanding, but I'm one of those people who can't rest until they have everything crystal clear." His face was a shadowy blur, but his stance revealed the same leashed tension she had heard in his voice. She was speaking with bulletlike rapidity, the words tumbling feverishly over each other. "If you'll just explain what Gunner meant, I'm sure it will—"

"Just what did Gunner say? I can hardly explain something away, if I don't know what it is."

"He called me . . . your lady."

He muttered a curse beneath his breath.

"I knew it was a mistake," she rushed on quickly. "I just didn't want to have it nagging at me."

"It's no mistake."

She turned to look at him. "What?" she whispered.

"The only mistake was Gunner's damn lack of discretion. I should have known he'd blow it."

"But he said—"

"That you're my lady? It's quite true. You are my lady, though I wouldn't have phrased it in just that fashion. Gunner's people have a rather simplistic view of the man-woman relationship. Still, the elemental fact exists that you do belong to me." He paused. "As I belong to you."

She shook her head dazedly. "This is insane. I just met you yesterday. We don't know anything about each other."

"I know everything about you."

"From Mark's letters? He couldn't have told you more than some basic facts." She laughed shakily. "And I can hardly believe that letters concerning someone as mundane as me would trigger any fantasies."

"I know everything about you," he repeated. "And I try not to fantasize about you at all. It disturbs me too much."

She couldn't breathe; the hot tingling in the pit of her stomach caused a muscular clenching that shocked her. No, she couldn't feel desire. It was something else. Not desire. Fear, amazement, anger. Not sexual hunger. Sex. The thought sent another shock jolting through her. Sex was a warm gentle river, not a rough, turbulent riptide. Sex was golden, kind Mark, not Jon Sandell. "No, Mark . . ."

"Mark is dead." Jon's words were harsh. "And if he wasn't, it still wouldn't matter. He had his turn. You're mine now."

"You keep saying that. I don't belong to anyone but myself." She ran her fingers distractedly through her hair. "And it's not true. I loved Mark. I don't love you."

"You will," he said with calm certainty.

"How can you be so sure? You may think you know everything about me, but I know nothing about you. Right now, I don't even think I like you very much."

"That's natural. I'm blasting you out of the complacent coccoon you've woven about yourself and Andrew. You're bound to resent it."

"I'm glad you're so understanding of my psychological quirks," she said tartly. "Freud, I presume?"

"Dzatskan, actually." For an instant there was a hint of humor in his voice. "But I didn't need his theories to tell me about you, Beth. We fit. You realize that as well as I do."

"No." Her voice was shaking. "You're not the kind of man I could ever care about. You're not . . ."

"Mark?" he finished for her. His hands suddenly gripped her shoulders with barely restrained violence. "For God's sake, give me a chance. I'll be better for you than Mark could ever have been."

"If you mean sex, there are other elements in a relationship I value more highly."

"I didn't mean sex. I'm talking about love, companionship, and everything that makes two people one."

"How can you talk about something we don't have? We're *strangers*, dammit."

"We're not . . ." His hands tightened on her shoulders. "I can't convince you, can I? Okay. Let's talk about the one aspect of our relationship even you can't deny. Let's talk about sex."

"I don't want to talk to you about any of this. I think I'll go inside."

"No, you started this discussion. Do you think I wouldn't have preferred to wait until you knew me better before we reached this point? I could have lied to you, but there's enough standing between us without that. I won't let anything stand between us from now on. Not even your fears. You may doubt our compatibility on every other level, but you know you're as sexually attracted to me as I am to you. Physically we're absolutely perfect for each other. There aren't another two people in a million who are as well suited sexually as we are."

"How can you know that's true? Do you have a crystal ball?"

He laughed mirthlessly. "Close. It doesn't matter how I know. All that matters is that you believe me. Sex between us will be absolutely incredible. It wouldn't matter if you hated my guts, I'd still be able to please you sexually."

"I *don't* believe you," she said fiercely. "I'm not the animal you think I am. I can't separate sex and love."

"Can't you?"

"No." She tugged futilely at his hands on her shoulders. Her throat was tight with emotion and she could barely get the words out. "Let me go. I can't stay here. . . ."

"I won't let you go. I can't let you go. You're a part of me. Shall I tell you what I want to do with you right now? I want to take you to bed and lose myself in you. I want you as naked and hungry as I am."

"You're crazy. I'm about to have a child."

"It doesn't make any difference. I'd take care not to hurt you or the baby. I could show you roads to pleasure you didn't know existed. Ways you were meant to travel only with me."

"Will you shut up! You're *frightening* me." The tears that were brimming in her eyes overflowed and ran down her cheeks. "I don't want to travel new roads. I don't want to be here in this strange house. I want to be home and safe and—"

He went still. "You're crying." His right hand left her shoulder and his fingers gently touched her cheek. "Oh, Lord, I didn't mean to upset you. Sometimes I get so damned frustrated I strike out at what's nearest, and there's no one nearer to me than you. Near to my heart, and my soul, and what I am." His arms enfolded her and his cold jaw pressed against her tear-stained cheek. He stroked her hair soothingly. "Forget it. I'm only a clumsy, blundering soldier who should know better than to put you through this right now."

The change in his demeanor from violent passion to paternal tenderness was as bewildering as what had preceeded it. Yet there was no doubting his sincerity. The web of tenderness in which he enveloped her was almost tangible, soothing her with the same tactile gentleness as his hand on her hair. She laughed shakily. "Forget it? How can I forget it?"

"Well, then don't forget it. I'm not sure I want you to dismiss it completely." His lips pressed her temple. "I like the idea of your looking at me and remembering how much I want you. Perhaps tonight, as you're lying in bed, you'll think about what I've said and imagine what it would be like to have me there with you. No, don't forget it. Just put it aside, and know my wanting you will never be a threat." He was rocking her gently. "It can only bring pleasure, Beth."

The snowflakes were falling around them in a lazy dreamlike tempo. She felt dreamlike, too, enfolded in darkness and strength and warmth. "I don't want this, Jon," she whispered. "You're not the kind of man I want to have in my life. There's too much violence in you. I can feel it all around me when I'm with you."

"All around you, but never touching you. That's why I'm here. So that you'll never know anything but gentleness and tranquillity."

Her answering laugh rang free and full of mirth. "I haven't noticed any great degree of tranquillity in the past two days of our acquaintance."

"Only because you've been fighting me at every turn. If you'd done what I told you to do, you wouldn't have had to confront Bardot or—"

"I hate people who say 'I told you so.' "

"I'll try to restrain myself in the future." His tone became grave. "In every way, Beth. I'm not as undisciplined as you might conclude. I won't force an intimacy between us that you're not ready for. I'm not about to rock the boat by scaring you away from me. I'll take anything you'll give me. Sex, companionship." He paused. "Love. Anything. The only thing I can't tolerate is for our relationship to stand still. I'm not a patient man."

"I suspected as much," she said dryly. "Of the choices I've been given, I'll opt for companionship."

"I was afraid you would." His tone was faintly rueful. "Pity. The other alternatives I gave you would have been much more interesting."

"And riskier. I told you I wasn't interested in taking chances. All I want is to be safe and keep Andrew safe."

He slowly released her and stepped back. "Then, that's what we'll shoot for. Friends?"

"Friends," she echoed softly.

"Now, I'd better get you inside and out of the cold." His big hand ruffled her hair teasingly. "You look like you're wearing a hood embroidered with snowflakes. You should have waited until I came in to have this discussion."

"I'm not very patient myself, and you didn't seem in any hurry to come back inside. You appeared absolutely fascinated by this winter wonderland."

"It *is* a wonderland." His hand beneath her elbow urged her toward the front door. As he opened it, an arrow of light illuminated his face. In that moment he didn't look hard or violent at all. His dark eyes were shining with eagerness as he studied the exquisite delicacy of a snowflake caught for a moment out of time on the wool of his sleeve. "So beautiful. I've read the pattern of a snowflake never repeats itself."

"I don't think anyone has ever gone to the trouble to take an in-depth survey." She gazed at him curiously. "You're staring at that snowflake as if you've never seen one before."

"I haven't. This is a first for me."

Her eyes widened. "Your first snowstorm? How odd."

The eagerness in his face was replaced by wariness. "Not so unusual. I grew up in desert country."

She nodded slowly. "But if you were abroad for so many years I don't see how you could have avoided running into snow somewhere. Where did you say you were stationed?"

"I didn't say." He shrugged. "I've batted around quite a bit, but principally in countries in the Southern Hemisphere."

"No wonder you've kept that wonderful tan. Mark's skin was that lovely bronze shade too. He grew up in a small town in New Mexico. Are you from New Mexico too?"

"We're from the same general area." Jon smiled as he closed the door. "You'd love my hometown, Beth. It's a place where you'd never have to worry about the cold or ice."

"It sounds wonderful." She shivered a little as she shrugged out of Gunner's jacket, opened the closet door, and reached for a hanger. "I visited Daytona, Florida, once and basked in the sun for two solid weeks. I loved every minute of it."

"Yet you came back to the North."

"I told you, my home is here. I believe in roots." She glanced at him over her shoulder as she hung up the jacket. "I guess that sounds very provincial to a world traveler like you."

"Why should it? It's usually the people who have no roots who miss them the most." His large hand closed over her smaller one, his fingers threading through her own. She felt a tiny unexpected shock that robbed her of breath and caused her gaze to meet his. The atmosphere in the last few minutes had been so light, almost casual, she had forgotten the tremendous physical rapport they shared. But he had not forgotten. His eyes were narrowed on her face with understanding and a touch of satisfaction. "You'll soon discover we have a good many other things in common."

"Will I?" She couldn't seem to tear her gaze away from his brilliant black eyes. The heat began to tingle and build within her and she forced herself to look away. "Well, I'm sure we have one thing in common. I'm absolutely starved. Shall we go and see if Gunner's managed to salvage dinner?"

The snow was falling more heavily now, Elizabeth noticed. It still hadn't escalated into a major storm, but it was proceeding rapidly in that direction. Standing in front of the floor-length windows in her bedroom was almost like being outside in the storm's midst. She pressed her palm to the glass. It was cold against her flesh. The contrast between the cold beneath her palm and the warmth of the room was pleasant, even faintly sensual.

She jerked her hand from the windowpane. Sensual. 'The adjective had popped into her mind with a naturalness that bewildered and frightened her. She had never thought of herself as a sensual person. Her sex life with Mark had been quite satisfactory. He had been an understanding and skillful lover, and their lovemaking had been very gentle and sweet. It had been a pleasant part of their marriage, but certainly not a major part. If her sensuality was to be aroused by anyone, surely it should have been with Mark, the man she loved. Not by Jon Sandell.

Yet she was compelled to admit she had been thrown into a fever of arousal more than once tonight. One moment she would be talking and laughing with Gunner and Jon, and the next she would be watching the smooth, coordinated litheness of Jon's movements as he crossed the room to stoke the logs in the fireplace. She would look up from pouring a cup of coffee and find her gaze clinging to the clean hard line of his lips. She would try to keep her gaze from his face and would focus on the lean strength of his hands, and wonder how those fingers would look against the paler flesh of her—

She closed her eyes. She didn't want this. She didn't want this aching between her thighs or the swelling sensitivity of her breasts. She didn't want to look at him and know he wanted her.

At no time during the evening had he been anything but the perfect companion. He had not betrayed by word or glance anything deeper than avuncular amusement and affection. Yet every minute she had been as conscious of his hunger for her as she had been on the deck outside a few hours earlier. He wanted her to be aware. He had said it himself. He wanted her to lie in bed tonight and think of him.

Well, she wouldn't do it. If she tried, she could block him out of her consciousness. She shrugged off the loose pink flannel robe and tossed it on the chair beside the window. She started to draw the yellow satin draperies closed, and then changed her mind. It would be soothing to watch the snow fall as she lay in bed. Better than counting sheep.

She slipped between the sheets and pulled the yellow coverlet up to her chin, her gaze fixed with lazy contentment on the falling snow beyond the window. She would go to sleep soon, and if she dreamed at all it would be of the child tucked beneath her heart. She would not permit Jon Sandell to invade her privacy.

The snow was a lovely lacy curtain sticking to the panes, each pattern totally unique. Who had said that? she wondered drowsily. Jon. She had a fleeting memory of his face as he glanced down at the snowflake. Eagerness, wonder, excitement. Such a little thing to become excited about.

Gunner Nilsen had betrayed the same joyous excitement as he blundered down the dangerous ski slope that afternoon. She would have to remember to ask Gunner tomorrow if he came from desert country too.

She nestled her cheek deeper into the softness of her pillow. The clean scent of starch and soap filled her nostrils, and the snow curtain was blurring before her eyes. The crackle of the burning logs in the fireplace was a soothing sound. She would *not* think about Jon Sandell. A few minutes more and she would be asleep, and the danger would be over.

The snow. There was something she should remember about the snow. Something that had been nibbling at her memory since she had seen Jon's expression as he looked down at the snowflake. But she wasn't going to think about Jon. Her lids refused to stay open any longer. She had won. Jon had lost.

Yet, had she won? She could see him so clearly even as she wavered on the edge of sleep. Jon standing at the window with his back to her watching the snow gather on the paddles of the mill wheel. His hands jammed in the pockets of the hunter-green wool robe she had bought for him, and on his face the same expression of wonder that had been there tonight. No, that was wrong. She had never bought a robe for Jon. It was Mark who had stood at the window of her bedroom over thirteen months ago gazing out at the first snow of the season. The memory that had eluded her was suddenly there before her. She had come up behind Mark and slipped her arm in his, murmuring something about the ice on the roads. He hadn't answered or made any comment but had continued to stare out the window for a long, long time with wonder and delight. Not Jon, but Mark. . . .

* * *

"You don't like this house, do you?"

Elizabeth looked from the modernistic painting over the fireplace to Jon sitting next to her on the couch. "Why do you say that? It's a very luxurious house. I've been very comfortable here this week."

"You were examining that painting as if it were a particularly repulsive cockroach."

She shrugged. "I don't like abstracts. I suppose it has something to do with my Yankee mentality. I have to have everything forthright and honest, no half-truths or subliminal perceptions." She studied the craggy boldness of his face. "I think you're a man who appreciates total honesty."

He glanced back at the painting and a faint smile curved his lips. "I thought I was at one time. Lately, I've found there are a hell of a lot of things that aren't what they seem to be at first glance." His gaze shifted back to the painting. "But it's not only the painting that bothers you. You aren't at ease here."

She should have known he'd sense the slight discomfort she was experiencing. He had appeared to be conscious of even her tiniest shift of mood during the past week. She felt his gaze on her with constant alertness as if it were vitally important that he observe and memorize everything she thought and did. She supposed it should have made her uncomfortable, but somehow it hadn't. Instead, she felt protected and treasured. How odd that a sense of perfect security could exist side by side with the intense sexual awareness between them.

Only a brilliant and extremely confident man could invoke and balance those two elements successfully. But then Jon *was* brilliant, and no one could doubt his self-confidence. She had also found he had a rapier wit and a passion for learning that was truly amazing. The intensity he possessed as one of his prime characteristics, became as irrepressible as the tide when channeled on any project or thought. The excellent library he had mentioned on the day they arrived was in constant use. A casual word to Jon could spark a search for knowledge that would last for hours or even days. His enthusiasm was utterly contagious, and she and Gunner found themselves constantly swept up and carried away by it. Though she had found out more than she ever wanted to know about stained glass, she thought ruefully. And all because she had remarked that the prismed sunlight pouring through the kitchen window reminded her of a Tiffany panel.

If Jon's driving intensity hadn't been tempered by a droll sense of humor, he would have been impossible to tolerate. Just when she was frustrated and ready to tell him where he could shove his precious research, he said something that made her laugh. The next minute she would find herself reaching for another encyclopedia or reference book and telling herself she was really doing this for herself, not the maddening man sitting at the desk across the library. After all, she had always wanted to know how stained glass was crafted.

It had been a week of learning for her in more ways than one. The long walks in the snow, the card games in the evening, these periods of peace and contentment in front of the fire after Gunner had gone to bed. They had all taught her facets of Jon Sandell she wouldn't have dreamed existed.

Jon's lips lifted in a lazy smile. "You're looking at me as if I've just been placed in the same category as the abstract."

"Was I?" Her brown eyes twinkled as she leaned back. "Well, you can't say you're either open or forthright. You've very definitely avoided revealing anything about your mysterious past." She held up her hand to stop him as he opened his mouth to speak. "Don't tell me. I know. I have to wait until after the baby is born. It doesn't bother me any longer. I'm getting accustomed to men of mystery trekking through my life. I certainly don't lie awake nights wondering if you're hired mercenaries or—"

"Really? What do you lie awake and wonder about?" he asked softly.

How your hands would feel on my naked breasts. How your tongue would feel on . . . The answer sprang full-blown into being. But she didn't wonder about those forbidden things. She very carefully kept herself from doing so. Her chest tightened and her tongue moistened her lower lip. "I don't wonder about anything. I go right to sleep as soon as my head hits the pillow."

His eyes gazing into her own were entirely too knowing. "Don't look now but your honest, uncompromising Yankee mentality just slipped a little."

"No such thing," she said crisply. "And it's not that I'm not at ease here, it's only that it's not home. All this sleek modern decor." Her gesture encompassed the room as well as the couch on which they were sitting. "I guess I prefer beautiful old furniture that has stood the test of time."

"Like the antiques at Mill Cottage? You place great value on the concept of home. Why is that?"

"Concept is such a cold word." She nibbled at her lower lip, trying to find the words. "And a home isn't cold at all. It's a place of tranquillity and love. When I was a child it was necessary for us to travel a lot. My mother was Denise Brandon, the concert pianist, and my father and I tried to accompany her whenever she went away on tour. We both hated to be away from the cottage, but it was better than being without my mother." Her face softened. "She was a very special person."

"I know," Jon said gently.

"You've heard of her? She became very well-known in the United States before she died, but she would never accept tours outside the country."

"I've heard of her."

Elizabeth fixed her gaze dreamily on the blue-red flames of the fire. "I hated to move from place to place, but it made coming home all the sweeter. I can remember sitting between my mother and father in the car driving down the road toward the cottage. With every mile I'd become more and more excited. First, we'd pass the white barn with advertising on the roof, then there were four Burma Shave signs before we came to the red silo. Finally, we'd cross the old covered bridge and I'd know we were almost home. I love that rickety old bridge. It's the last link between the strange and the familiar. The last bridge home."

"The last bridge home," Jon repeated. "I like that."

There was a long lazy silence in the room, the only sound was the hiss and crackle of the burning logs.

"You do know I love you." Jon's voice was low, his gaze still on the flames.

She stiffened, jarred out of her cozy euphoria. "You couldn't, it's not possible."

"It's impossible not to love you. You're warm and generous and loving. You fill me with laughter and lust and tenderness. There's not a second of the day or night I don't want to spend with you. There's not a moment of my future I don't want to share with you."

She closed her eyes as waves of emotion washed over her. "No, it's too soon. It couldn't happen."

"I love you," he said again with absolute certainty.

He meant it. The knowledge caused the turmoil within her to take on added dimensions. She opened her eyes. "I don't love you. I may never love you."

"Yes, you will. You're already coming close." His gaze lifted from the fire to her face. A loving smile lit his rough-hewn face with rare masculine beauty. "Don't worry about it now. I just thought you should know."

She laughed shakily. "So you dropped it casually into the conversation."

"Not casually. Nothing is casual where you're concerned, Beth." Something flickered in the brilliant darkness of his eyes. "But I'm trying to be gentle and civilized at the moment. It's not easy for me. By nature I'm not a particularly civilized man."

No, it wouldn't be easy for Jon Sandell to temper his bold warrior instincts. Yet for her sake he was making every effort to do it. The realization touched her poignantly. "There's too much standing between us. Too many things I don't know."

"They'll be gone soon." His index finger brushed her cheekbone. "Then there will be nothing between us more weighty than these freckles."

"Perhaps. You'd know better than I." The pad of his finger was gentle and caressing on her skin. She wanted to tilt her head, lean closer, offer more. "You're the one with all the secrets."

His eyes were studying her expression. "You like me to touch you, don't you? I told you that we matched. I'm aching to have your hands on me."

"No, I—"

His fingers moved to cover her lips. "Hush, I'm not rushing you. I'm being civilized, remember? I can wait." He paused before adding in a tone a level above a whisper, "Maybe." His thumb rubbed slowly, sensuously, over her lower lip.

Her lips parted. They were swollen, throbbing beneath his thumb. Her breasts lifted and fell with every breath. She felt as if each nerve in her body were sensitized to an acute pitch, and yet a languid heat invaded every muscle. She leaned slowly forward, her gaze clinging helplessly to his face. "Jon, this is crazy."

She wanted him. The flush suffusing her cheeks, the glistening brown of her eyes, the soft pliancy of her body. All the signs were there. He could reach out and take what he wanted. He could pleasure her and, at least for a little while, she would forget suspicion. Perhaps she would even forget Mark. How he wanted her. He ached. He throbbed. The muscles of his stomach were knotted, ready. *He* was ready.

But she wasn't ready. Not yet. What she wanted now might not be what she would want tomorrow, and he wasn't interested in a one-night stand. He needed tomorrow, he needed forever.

Jon's fingers fell away from her lips. "It's even worse than crazy. You were right. It's too soon." He tried to steady his uneven breathing. "And, Lord, I wish it wasn't."

She stared at him blankly.

A crooked smile twisted the corner of his lips. "You're not the only one who's surprised." She made a motion to pull away from him. He stopped her. "No, don't leave me.'

"I think it's time I went to bed."

He thought so too. It was time she went to his bed. Time she slept in his arms. He would be exquisitely gentle and . . .

"Stay with me," he urged softly. He drew her close, pressing her silky brown head against his shoulder. "Just sit here with me and watch the fire. That's not much to ask."

As Elizabeth slowly relaxed against him, she wasn't sure that was true. On the surface his request was innocuous, but she had the feeling he was winning more by restraint than he ever would with aggression. The wool of his sweater was slightly rough against her cheek, his hand stroking her hair was infinitely soothing, and the scent of soap and musk blended subtly with the aromatic odor of burning pine.

Lord, he was hurting. He concentrated on trying to block out the sensations tearing him apart, forcing each muscle to relax. It took three minutes to remove the visible signs of his arousal. Desire still existed, but at least she wouldn't be aware of it. She would feel safe. And, if he was lucky, tonight would be another step forward. Another mile traveled on the long way home.

Five

"What the hell are you doing?" There was exasperation as well as amusement in Jon's expression as he gazed at Elizabeth lying on her back in the snow, her arms flung wide.

"Making angels." Her tongue was caught between her teeth as she briskly flapped her arms back and forth. "Now, hush. I haven't the breath to do this and talk to you too. I feel as if Andrew's lying right on top of one of my lungs this morning."

Gunner looked up after he'd inserted the second pinecone eye in his snowman. "That looks like fun, maybe we could make an entire chain of angel imprints in a circle around my snowman and—"

"No, Gunner." Jon stepped forward and pulled Elizabeth to her feet. He turned her around and began to brush the snow from her coat and slacks. "You're as bad as she is. How long have you two been out here? She's wet to the skin."

"Since breakfast." Gunner was frowning with concern as he looked at Elizabeth. "Is she really damp? Lord, I'm sorry. She seemed to be having so much fun I guess I didn't think."

"You seldom do." The sarcasm in Jon's tone was biting.

"Be quiet, Jon." Elizabeth's brown eyes were dancing as she glanced at him over her shoulder. "You're just crabby because we were having fun and you were left out. It's all your own fault. If you'd gotten out of bed at a respectable hour instead of sleeping until almost noon, you'd have been able to come out and play too. We've had a perfectly splendid snowball fight, and Gunner has made the largest snowman in the history of New York State."

Gunner grinned. "Only New York? I was hoping that at the very least I'd beaten the North American record."

Elizabeth tilted her head and regarded the eight-foot snowman critically. "I don't know . . . There are some ice sculpture aficionados in Minnesota who'd be pretty tough competition."

"Ice and snow are not the same," Gunner said with royal hauteur. "I will not be subject to an unfair comparison."

Elizabeth's laugh rang out on the clear, cold air, and Jon experienced a pang of pleasure. How he loved to hear her laugh. The sound of her laughter was low and sweet and brimming with robust joyousness. Her face sparkled and her skin bloomed with a silky sheen. His throat tightened helplessly as he gazed at her. *She* was blooming. Her skin, her body, the tousled silk of her straight brown hair. All blooming. All radiant. Elizabeth.

"You'd better go inside and change," he said gruffly, when he'd finally managed to tear his gaze away from her.

Elizabeth wrinkled her nose at him. "Spoilsport. Just for that we won't let you help name our magnificent creation. What do you think, Gunner? He looks terribly wise. Solomon?"

Gunner shook his head. "Too pompous. You can be wise without being boring."

Jon suddenly felt very old and jaded. They were both so damn young and beautiful and full of the elixir of life. Last night in front of the fire he had been full of hope, but today he was bombarded by doubt. When had he last been able to shrug off responsibility and just enjoy himself? Hell, he couldn't even remember when he had last let his burdens slide.

"What about Benjamin Franklin? He had a sense of humor," Elizabeth suggested. "And he came from good Yankee stock, which is import—" She broke off as she shot a mischievous glance at Jon and saw his expression. The grin immediately faded from her face, and it clouded with concern. "Jon, is something wrong?" She took an impulsive step toward him. "I didn't mean—" She stopped short as the world began to whirl around her in a blur of white and cerulean blue. "Jon!"

"God!" In two strides Jon was beside her. He lifted her into his arms and pressed her against his chest. "Pains?"

"No." She shook her head. To her relief the world

was steadying itself once again. "I was just dizzy for a moment. You can let me go now."

"The hell I will." He strode toward the lodge with her. His face was pale beneath his tan. Almost as pale as Benjamin Franklin's, she thought hazily. "You're going to bed to rest. Gunner, if you can tear yourself away from your artistic endeavors, you might make some hot tea for her."

"Right away." Gunner passed them at a run, bounding up the stairs of the deck. "She didn't eat much breakfast. I'll fix her a light lunch."

"For heaven's sake, it was only a dizzy spell," she protested. "It's perfectly natural for a woman in my condition to have her hormones go crazy at a time like this. I probably changed positions too quickly when you jerked me to my feet."

"So now it's my fault," he said between his teeth as he climbed the steps of the deck. "I did *not* jerk you. I helped you to your feet."

Her eyes twinkled up at him. "You helped me," she agreed. "Forcefully."

"I didn't—" He drew an uneven breath. "Save your breath, and rest, dammit." They were inside the lodge, and he was climbing the stairs to the second floor. "You shouldn't have been out wallowing in the snow anyway. Don't you have any sense?"

"I wasn't wallowing. I was creating." She giggled. "Though I admit from an observer's point of view it might have been difficult to differentiate the two. The exercise was good for me. I haven't been able to get out much in the last week."

Jon didn't answer but his lips tightened grimly. A moment later he carefully negotiated the door to her bedroom and kicked it shut behind him. He crossed the room and deposited her on the bed.

She immediately started to get up. "I'm all wet. Let me change before I get the coverlet damp."

"Sit still." He shrugged off his coat, tossed it carelessly on the floor, and knelt in front of her. His fingers trembled slightly as he unbuttoned her navy coat and slipped it from her shoulders. He drew the thigh-length, cable-knit sweater over her head and threw it on the floor beside his coat. "Lord, even your blouse is wet." He rose to his feet. "I'll be right back. Take off your boots and socks."

She made a face at the bathroom door as it closed behind him. Jon's dominant streak was emerging with a vengeance. Oh, well, it wouldn't hurt to indulge him. Perhaps it would make up for the hurt she had unintentionally inflicted upon him earlier. When she had turned and seen the expression on his face, she had been filled with such empathy it had shocked her. What could he have been thinking about, to cause that look on his face? She began to work at removing her suede boots. The wet snow had turned their pale beige color to a shade of dark brown. She was damper than she realized. The vigorous activity she'd engaged in all morning had kept her from being conscious of either the damp or the cold.

The door opened and Jon came back into the bedroom with several large white towels draped over his arm. He stopped by the closet and slid open the door. "The towels are warm from the heated rack. If they don't get rid of the chill, I'll put you in the shower."

Her eyes widened. "I don't think that will be necessary."

He jerked a caftan that was the color of orange sherbet from a hanger, and came back to where she sat. "We'll see." He knelt before her, his fingers undoing the buttons of her blouse. "Believe me, I'd like to avoid it as much as you. I'm afraid you'd get dizzy again. Which means I'd have to join you in the shower." He pushed the blouse from her shoulders, his hands going to the front fastening of her bra. "And who knows where that might lead."

She looked down at his fingers, as he struggled to undo the fastening. His hands were strong and tanned against the white lace garment. Strong, and yet trembling. Her breath caught in her throat and a tiny quiver shook her.

"You're shivering. Are you cold?" His gaze lifted to her face, and he inhaled sharply. "No, you're not cold . . ."

"No," she whispered. Heat was throbbing through every vein. She could feel the flush that rose to her cheeks and throat. His knuckles were resting against her full breasts that were also flushed, engorged, aching.

He closed his eyes. "Not now. Don't do this to me now. I thought I had it under control. It took me most of the damn night but I thought . . ." His eyes opened. Burning. Brilliant. Hungry. "You're not well. I can't . . ."

"I'm fine." She could barely get the words past the dryness in her throat. How had she come this far in so short a time? The words she had spoken were an invitation to intimacy.

He shook his head with a touch of desperation. "No."

"I'm not very attractive right now." She laughed shakily. "And about as graceful as a rhinoceros."

"Not attractive at all," he said huskily. "Beautiful." His palms moved down to rest on her abdomen. "This is beautiful. Tight and brimming and full of life. And your breasts . . ."

She looked up from where his hands lay so close to her breasts. "They ache. I ache. Do you suppose you could just hold me?" she asked softly.

His eyes were smoky and glazed as he gazed at her. "Yes, I can do that. It's going to come close to killing me, but I can do it." Jon's mouth was coming closer. She could feel his warm breath on her lips. His hand moved from her abdomen to pull her close against him. His chest was moving erratically with the harshness of his breathing and the pulse in his temple was throbbing hard, fast. He was being so tender. She wanted to bury her fingers in his hair and bring him even closer to her. She sat there, every muscle tense, her breath, too, coming shallowly.

His tongue tasted her. Warm. Wet. Erotic.

A shudder ran through her. She gasped against his lips, and swayed toward him, bonelessly pliant. It was as if his lips were jerking hot cords somewhere within her.

"You'll be more comfortable if we lie down." He gently pushed her backward on the sunshine-yellow satin of the spread. His fingers were running through her hair, but she was barely conscious of his action. His mouth held all her attention. She raised her mouth mindlessly toward his as she gave a low cry. The sensation was indescribable, his mouth hard, and yet gentle, his tongue moving rhythmically to caress her own. She was lost in the intimacy of the kiss, knowing she'd never before shared so much of herself, given so much of herself through the simple, yet passionate, act of kissing. Jon seemed to tap feelings and emotions in her that before now had lain dormant.

She was trembling when Jon finally ended the kiss. He began to make lazy circles on her abdomen with his palm, and the incredible tenderness in his action made her realize she'd never have thought him capable of such warmth. She felt as if she were being torn apart by her conflicting emotions. Her tongue moistened her lips as she raised her head from Jon's shoulder. "Jon," she murmured.

"I told you there was something special between us." There was a hint of satisfaction in his hoarse voice. "Only with me. We're going to be perfect together. You will never respond to anyone but me in this way," he said quietly. She made an attempt to sit up.

"No." He quickly stilled her. "Stay here. Let me get you whatever you need. You have to be very careful, you've had a very full morning."

He was being so sensitive, so thoughtful. She wanted to give him an indication of how her feelings for him had changed in so short a time. Reaching to trace the outline of his mouth with her finger, she watched his dark eyes as they glowed down at her, his expression as intense as his lips had been when they'd moved over hers.

Withdrawing her finger, she closed her eyes and tried to settle herself down comfortably in the bed, but she was so tired suddenly, that it was difficult to think of moving even a muscle. She didn't have to move, however, because in an instant Jon was doing everything. Removing the rest of her clothes, running heated towels over her body, slipping the velvet robe over her head. "Sit up, love. Just for a minute." She sat up, watching dreamily as he put her arms in the sleeves of the caftan, lifting her to pull the gown down. His lips brushed her forehead as he pulled the yellow coverlet up around her. "Better?"

Better. That was the understatement of the century, perhaps the millennium. She was deliciously content, lost in an afterhaze of pleasure. "Wonderful."

"I'm glad." He rose jerkily to his feet. "I'll go see what's keeping Gunner."

"I'm glad something kept him," Elizabeth said dreamily. "Or I wouldn't have had the opportunity to realize how—" She stopped, her eyes widening with distress. Jon's face was taut, the skin pulled tight over his cheekbones. Lines of pain were visible on each side of his mouth. "Oh, Jon, I'm sorry. What a selfish bitch you must think me." How cruel she had been. She had known Jon wanted her and yet she had taken his tenderness and comfort, never considering the price it had cost him.

He shook his head. "No, this was your time. I wanted it that way." He grimaced. "But fortunately, since you'll be here at the lodge for a while longer, I'll be able to convince you there's no turning back for us now."

Jon's hands clenched at his sides. He was silent for a moment, struggling for control. "There will be another time. I can wait." He turned and walked toward the door.

"Jon."

He paused with his hand on the doorknob. "Yes?"

"There *will* be another time. I promise you." She smiled at him with a loving joyousness that made his heart give a little jerk. "And I think Andrew likes you. You notice he didn't protest at all when you touched me so tenderly."

For a moment a flicker of a smile lighted the tenseness of his expression. "I know he likes me. Why not? He's obviously a boy of impeccable taste."

The door closed softly behind him.

Elizabeth stared at the door, the smile lingering contentedly on her lips. The room was suddenly very lonely without Jon's vital presence. There were so many aspects to his complex personality. Gentleness, intelligence, passion, possessiveness. Every passing day uncovered another intricate layer. As soon as she began to fathom one facet, it would change and be transformed into something else. He was a man who couldn't bear to stand still. He had told her that himself. And he would certainly never be easy to understand.

Andrew stirred beneath her heart, and she laughed softly. "Hello. You've been very lazy to-day." She lay there, wrapped in warmth and another feeling. A feeling she didn't wish to label. "He says you like him," she whispered. "I hope that's true, because I'm afraid your mother is . . ." She didn't finish the sentence, even in her own mind. To complete it would mean a commitment, and there was no hurry. She would let herself be carried along on a sweet silver stream of emotion. Jon would let nothing hurt her. Not even himself.

Jon leaned back against the door, as aching need racked his body. Perspiration beaded his forehead as he concentrated all his energy on subduing the hunger tearing at him like a ravenous animal. Close. It had been so close. He could still taste her on his tongue. He could still see her lying on the yellow satin. He could smell her perfume. He smothered a groan.

"Jon?"

Gunner stood at the head of the stairs, a covered rattan tray in his hands. His dark blue eyes were troubled.

Jon straightened. "I was just coming down to see what was keeping you."

Gunner strolled toward him. "I dallied a bit. I had a feeling I'd be interrupting something." He smiled gently. "And I never ignore my instincts. They've saved my neck too often."

Gunner's instincts had saved Jon's neck a time or two as well. "I'm going for a walk. See that Elizabeth has a good lunch and takes a nap." He moved jerkily down the hall. His muscles felt as if they were encased by barbed wire. "Did you radio Barnett this morning?"

Gunner nodded. "No sign of Bardot in the area. We still have him running around in circles."

"Good." Jon edged past Gunner and started down the stairs. "I want to talk to Barnett when I get back. It's time we set up the refuge. I have to discuss a meeting with Alex Ben Raschid."

"I'll tell him to stand by for your call. When will you be back?"

Hours. Days. How long would it take to uncoil the hunger inside him? He had always had absolute control over his body. Until now. "Give me two hours."

A frown darkened Gunner's face. "Be careful; another blizzard is moving in."

He would welcome a blizzard. It would give him something to fight beside the rigid pain in his loins. "I'll watch out for it." He looked back over his shoulder. "You just keep an eye on Elizabeth. No more romping in the snow."

"I wouldn't think of it." Gunner's lips were twitching as he reached Elizabeth's door. "I'm sure the lady has . . . er . . . 'romped' quite enough for today."

Elizabeth awoke after midnight to find a dampness between her thighs. Panic rose within her.

"No!" Her cry was a cross between a whimper and a frustrated groan. She struggled to a sitting position, her gaze going to the wall of windows across the room. The snow hurling itself against the glass seemed to be a solid blanket rather than individual snowflakes, and the wind was moaning like a lost child. "Not now, Andrew!"

She managed to get up from the bed. A nagging ache in her lower abdomen only increased her panic. "No wonder you were so lazy today. You were saving all your energy for this, you rascal." She crossed the room, opened the door, and went out into the hall. "Jon, Gunner, get up. We have to go the hospital."

Gunner's door opened immediately. His blond hair was tousled, and he was hurriedly tying the belt of a wine-colored robe. "The baby?"

"My water broke. We have to get to the hospital. Where's Jon?"

"I don't think he's gone to his room yet. He was still in the library when I came upstairs."

"What's wrong?" Jon asked. He was mounting the steps two at a time, and she turned to him in relief. Jon was here. Everything would be fine now. She tried to smile. "Andrew decided he was tired of waiting. We have to get to the hospital right away."

"Andrew!" Jon was beside her in seconds, scooping her up and heading back down the hall toward her room. "Get clean sheets and towels from the hall closet downstairs."

"Right." Gunner was already barreling down the stairs.

"Jon, put me down. You don't understand." Elizabeth was struggling helplessly in Jon's arms as he carried her across the room and set her down on the bed. "We have to hurry. It will take us hours to get to the hospital in this storm."

"Listen, Beth." Jon's expression was grave as he met her eyes. "We can't risk it. Just look at that storm." He nodded toward the windows. "The roads are bound to be closed. We couldn't get through without a snowplow."

"We could try. Andrew—"

"Andrew will be far safer here than in the truck. What if we got stranded out there? You might have to give birth in the truck and then we'd have the problem of getting a newborn baby safely through the storm to shelter." His hand cupped her chin, and his voice was velvet with gentleness. "I won't risk either you or the child. You'll give birth to Andrew here where I can make sure you're both warm and secure."

Her gaze went to the storm raging outside the windows again. He was right. She knew he was right, but it didn't stem the panic and frustration she was experiencing. Why now? She had wanted to give birth to Andrew surrounded by doctors and nurses in an antiseptic, sterile environment. She wanted her son to have every chance at survival.

"I'm frightened," she whispered. "Nothing must happen to my baby, Jon. I couldn't bear it."

"Nothing's going to happen to either of you," he said gently. "*I* couldn't bear it." His index finger pressed her nose teasingly. "So I'm going to make sure mother and child are going to do fabulously well."

He was so confident her spirits began to rise buoyantly in response. "And how do you intend to accomplish this feat? Neither you nor Gunner are doctors." She made a face. "Or maybe you are. For all I know, you could be anything or anyone."

"I'm afraid not, but as part of our training we've witnessed childbirth before, and we're two fairly intelligent men. We'll manage between us. I've been reading up on it lately. It's all very basic."

"Basic," she repeated. "Well, I agree with your

choice of words." She shook her head. "You've actually been researching the art of midwifery?"

He shrugged. "We were trained to be prepared for any eventuality. There was a book in the library written by a nurse who had extensive experience as a midwife in the Belgian Congo. The subject has interested me since I saw my first live birth."

"Well, it's certainly more practical than how to fashion stained glass," she said faintly. "Remind me to ask you about your 'training' when I'm feeling a bit better, and do me a favor and keep the manual handy. For heaven's sake, don't wing it."

"I promise. Strictly by the book. Now, let me help you get out of these clothes." His hands were on the hem of her gown. "Are you in any pain?"

"Not yet. I was aching a little when I woke up, but it's gone now." She helped him pull the gown over her head. "This is getting to be a habit. I always thought I was a modest person, but I seem to be taking this very calmly."

"There isn't time for modesty and why should you feel uncomfortable? There's only Gunner and me, and we care more about you than any doctor possibly could." He kissed her cheek as he pulled the sheet up about her shoulders. "Gunner is your good friend and I'm the man who is going to love and watch over you for the rest of your life."

"It's not fair for you to sneak that in," she protested. "I don't want to have to worry about anything but Andrew right now. You're catching me at a very vulnerable moment."

"I know." His dark eyes were twinkling. "I figured I should get something out of this. I'm about to go through a traumatic experience."

"*You* are! I'm the one who—" She began to chuckle helplessly. "Just go get that damn manual. I hope to heaven the copyright isn't in the seventeenth century."

"I think you're safe there. I don't believe the copyright office was founded until—" He broke off as she gasped and suddenly bent over in pain. The lightness vanished from his face. "The pain is back?"

It was a moment before the spasm subsided and she was able to answer. "Oh, yes, it's back. I believe Master Andrew's entrance into the world is going to prove difficult."

His hand smoothed the hair away from her face. "We'll just have to do something about that. These young whippersnappers have to learn to respect their mothers." He stood up, his gaze on her face. "I'll be right back. I won't let you suffer."

"I understand a certain amount of discomfort goes with the territory."

"It shouldn't." His voice was rough. "It's stupid for you to have to suffer like this. I won't tolerate it."

She felt a surge of maternal tenderness that had nothing to do with Andrew. "Okay, wave your magic wand and banish it into the great beyond. I'll be glad to cooperate." Pain twisted inside her and she cried out before she could stifle it. She felt a bead of perspiration run down the side of her face. "Very glad," she muttered, closing her eyes.

She heard him utter a low curse that was quite

satisfyingly obscene. She could have muttered a few curses herself at that moment. She heard the door open and her eyelids flew open. "I just thought of something. Couldn't you use the shortwave radio and get a doctor to talk you through the birth? I saw something on television once—" She stopped. He was shaking his head. "Why not?"

His gaze shifted from her face to the window. "I was trying to get a weather report earlier this evening and the radio was dead as a doornail. It could be the unit or the weather." He shrugged. "Who knows? At any rate, the bottom line is that you'll have to trust me." His gaze returned to her. "You won't be sorry, Beth."

She suddenly knew he was right. She could place her trust in him without reservation. He would never betray that trust. "I imagine we'll muddle through together." Her lips were trembling as she smiled at him. "I do trust you, Jon."

He opened his lips to say something and then closed them without speaking. "I'll try to find you a sedative to help the pain. I think I have something that will do the trick."

By the time he and Gunner returned ten minutes later, her pains were coming much closer together and racking her body with spasms. She tried to remember what she had read about natural childbirth. Breathing. That was it; she was supposed to breath rhythmically. She should have gone to the childbirth classes at the clinic in Albany, but there had been that data processing prerequisite she needed, and it was given only on Mondays and . . .

"Beth, open your eyes. You have to drink this. It will make you feel better." Jon was kneeling beside her, a glass of milk in his hand. His dark eyes were gazing intently into her own. Gentleness, warmth, love. They were all there and something more. Safety and surcease from all pain and fear.

"It's not too strong, is it? I think I'm supposed to push."

"You'll be perfectly clearheaded." He was holding her head carefully, the rim of the glass pressing her lips. "I've just added a sedative I brought back with me from abroad." His gaze was holding her own. "It's very safe and said to be a miracle drug. You'll have no pain at all from now on. You'll be absolutely relaxed and the baby will come easily, joyously. Do you believe me?"

Of course she believed him. It was clear everything he said was true. It would be wonderful to be free of pain. She nodded and quickly swallowed the milk. It was warm and soothing and thoroughly disgusting. "I hate hot milk."

Jon chuckled. "But the pain is gone."

It *was* gone and she wasn't even surprised. "You bet it is." She grinned up at him. "Shall we get this show on the road? Andrew is getting impatient."

She heard Gunner's delighted laughter and laughed back at him over Jon's shoulder. She was jubilantly, vibrantly alive and so happy. So very happy.

Jon smiled at both of them. "I guess we'll start at chapter one of the manual: 'Cleansing the Patient Thoroughly.' "

Andrew Ramsey was born at 3:42 A.M. during the worst blizzard to hit the state of New York in fifty years. Her son had his father's golden hair and her brown eyes, and when Jon put him in her arms she knew beyond the shadow of a doubt the meaning of happiness. Happiness was Andrew.

"He smells so sweet. What did you powder him with?" Her lips brushed the top of the baby's head. His skin was soft as slipper satin against her lips. She had always thought the comparison trite, but nothing came closer to the glowing freshness.

"Your talcum." Gunner smiled down at her with weary satisfaction. "The rest is strictly improvised, diapers from pillowcases, swaddling blanket from sheets. I haven't decided what to do about a cradle yet. I'll set up a nursery in the guest room next door so I can watch over him and let you get the rest you need."

"Perhaps we can pick up a cradle when we take him to the hospital for a checkup." She was still looking down at Andrew and didn't see the glance the two men exchanged. "And we'll definitely need some disposable diapers."

"I'll put them first on the list," Gunner said lightly.

"Not quite," Jon said. "Bottles and formula should take precedence, I think. Why don't you see what you can rustle up from the cellar in the way of an adequate-size bottle and rubber to fashion a nipple?"

"Why should he do that?" Elizabeth drew the baby closer. "I'm going to breast-feed him. I've never intended doing anything else. Most of the books I've read say it's better psychologically for a child to be breast-fed in infancy."

Something flickered in Jon's eyes. "I hear sometimes it can be . . . inconvenient."

"Nonsense, I'm going to breast-feed him," she said firmly.

"So it appears." Jon's expression was totally shuttered as he gazed down at her. Then he smiled. "I guess you're not going to need us for that little operation."

"I can handle it myself." Elizabeth felt as if she could handle the sun, the moon, and the entire NASA space program at the moment. "You go see what you can do about Andrew's cradle."

Jon shot an amused sideways glance at Gunner. "Dismissed?"

Gunner nodded mournfully. "Cast aside the moment a new man appears on the scene. How fickle can you get?"

Elizabeth lifted her eyes from the "new man" and slowly shook her head. A smile so loving it was blindingly radiant touched her lips. "Oh, no. Don't think you two will ever get away from me. After what we've gone through together you're both *mine* now. My family." Her gaze returned to her son as he lay in the bend of her arm. "Andrew's family. You're officially adopted."

"Then I guess we'd better see about that cradle." Jon's voice was husky. "Come on, Gunner. You're the expert on improvisation."

Elizabeth didn't look up when they left the room.

The two men were silent as they walked slowly down the stairs. It wasn't until they reached the foyer that Gunner said softly, "I feel as if I've just been knighted. It was kind of . . . wonderful."

Jon nodded. "Though I didn't expect her to want to breast-feed Andrew. I suppose I should have realized she'd react that way. It's going to cause problems."

Gunner smiled. "Do you care?"

Not if it makes her happy. Not if it makes her smile as she had just before they left the room. "No, it doesn't matter. I'll deal with it later."

That problem would undoubtedly be minor in comparison to the others looming on the horizon. His instincts weren't as finely tuned as Gunner's, but he had a hunch their peaceful hiatus was almost at an end.

Six

"Did you have a nice walk?" Gunner placed the baby carefully in Elizabeth's arms, then smiled as he looked up and saw her wind-flushed cheeks and sparkling eyes. "Yes, I can see you did."

"It was fine. Was Andrew all right?"

"A perfect gentleman. I know this will be a terrible blow to your maternal ego, but we got along splendidly without you for the past hour. Andrew and I understand each other."

"That's because you both have the mind of a child," Jon drawled. "Direct, easily amused, and stubborn as hell."

"Ouch." Gunner made a face. "I won't stand here and be maligned. I'm going back to the library and finish the book I started reading to Andrew."

"What were you reading? *The Little Engine That Could?*" Elizabeth asked with a grin. "I hate to disillusion you, but I don't think he's ready for such weighty literature yet. After all, he's only three weeks old."

Gunner shook his head. "Certainly not. I wouldn't think of insulting him with that pap. We're perusing Einstein's Theory of Relativity at the moment." He turned away and started down the hall. "Tomorrow we may start studying philosophy. Socrates might intrigue . . ." His words trailed off as he disappeared into the library.

Elizabeth stared after him in bemusement. "Do you suppose he's really reading Einstein's theories to Andrew?"

"I wouldn't put it past him," Jon said with a smile. "Gunner is capable of anything."

"But he's wonderful with Andrew." She glanced down at her son, and her smile was replaced by a frown of distress. "He's not eating properly. I *know* Andrew should be eating more than he does. The first two weeks after his birth he was absolutely ravenous, but this last week he's skipped his night feeding entirely and doesn't seem to be interested in the afternoon feeding either. I think he's sick."

"He couldn't be ill. He's growing by leaps and bounds," Jon said with comforting certainty. "There's no way you can say he's wasting away."

"No." Andrew was enchantingly plump and appeared to be growing in strength with every passing day. That was why his sudden aversion to nourishment was so puzzling . . . and frightening. "What if he stops eating entirely? What if—" She stopped. "We must get him to a doctor."

"You know we can't do that. The roads are still closed due to the last storm." Jon's voice was soothing. "And I'm sure there's nothing seriously wrong with the child. Have you thought about the possibility of an allergy? I've heard of rare cases in which a baby is allergic to his mother's milk. You might consider trying one of the formulas listed in the midwife manual."

"I guess I'll have to," she said dejectedly. "At this rate, I won't have any milk to give him anyway. We've got to get out of here. It's not safe for Andrew, for us, to be cut off without any way to communicate with the outside world. Is Gunner still working on the radio?"

"He thinks it needs a part."

"And he can't get a part until the roads are clear. It's a vicious circle."

"Vicious is a hard word," Jon said gently. "And I was under the impression you've been quite content these last few weeks."

She had been marvelously content. Her recovery from childbirth was unusually speedy and she had been up and around within three days. Andrew was a wondrous spring of delight and she had been so absorbed in her son that all her aches and pains had faded into the background. Jon had almost had to pry her forcibly away from Andrew so she could rest every afternoon.

Jon. She felt a warm glow spread through her as she looked at him. No one could have been kinder, or gentler, or more understanding. She was conscious that he had subdued any hint of his desire for her. He seemed to sense she needed this time to become acquainted with her son and accustom herself to her new role. He had told her he wasn't a patient man, but he had been more than patient with her.

"I've been very happy," she said softly. "Andrew's wonderful and you and Gunner have been so kind. It's been like being enclosed in a sparkling bubble that lets in all the beautiful colors but filters out everything worrisome and ugly. I've been floating up and up, higher every day."

"I'd like to keep you in that bubble." There was a sadness in Jon's eyes that puzzled her. "Unfortunately, the chance of that occurring doesn't look very promising."

Bardot. The thought of the government man rudely intruded into her beautiful bubble of security. She hadn't thought of him since Andrew arrived. She had shut him out with the other disturbing influences she knew she eventually would have to face. But she couldn't be bothered about Bardot yet, not when she had the problem of Andrew's lack of appetite to worry about. "Why did you have to pick a place in the middle of nowhere? Andrew—"

"Andrew is a fine, healthy boy, and he's going to stay that way. Now put him back to bed, and let him take his nap."

"All right. Just as soon as he's had his bath. Will you be coming up?"

"I'll have to pass. There's something else I have to do."

She tried to mask the twinge of disappointment she felt at the tiny rejection. She had grown accustomed to having Jon around constantly, and she knew he enjoyed Andrew's bath time as much as she did. She forced herself to smile. "Whatever you say, but Andrew will be most insulted at the slight."

"I'll make it up to him."

He watched until she reached the top of the stairs, and then turned on his heel and walked swiftly toward the library.

Andrew was sound asleep in her arms by the time Elizabeth reached the nursery. Lord, he was beautiful. She stood looking at him in blissful admiration for a few moments after she had put him in the heavily padded drawer that served as his makeshift crib. She was so lucky to have him. She gently caressed his soft cheek with her finger. She couldn't bear to wake him, the bath could wait. Perhaps Jon would be free later to enjoy it with her.

"Get me Barnett." Jon's voice was savage as he strode into the library. "We're going to get out of here. I'll be damned if I'll stay here and lie to her any longer. I feel worse than a Judas."

Gunner looked up from the book he was reading and rose to his feet. He moved quickly toward the radio on the long, modern table against the wall. "I was wondering when you were going to break. I'll be glad to have it finished, too, but it may take a few days. Ben Raschid insists on his man, Clancy Donahue, handling the security arrangements. It's going to be a very delicate transaction moving Elizabeth and Andrew from U.S. soil without a ripple of suspicion. Barnett tried to convince him it would be no problem for us, but the sheik is a very determined man."

"That's why he was chosen." Jon should have expected this holdup, but it was annoying nevertheless. He wanted it *over*. His temperament wasn't suited to deceit, particularly when that deceit involved Elizabeth. "Donahue better be damn quick or I'll give orders for us to handle the transfer ourselves."

Gunner pursed his lips in a soundless whistle. He had been aware of Jon's growing frustration, but he hadn't thought it had reached such an explosive level. "Do you think she's ready to hear it?"

"No." Jon's lips tightened. "But we're going to tell her anyway. She may never be ready to accept the truth, but we've got to try. It's better than continuing to manipulate her."

"All right, it's your decision." Gunner turned and clicked on the radio. "And I'm glad as hell I didn't have to make it."

The two men were in the middle of transmitting a message on the radio, when Elizabeth walked into the library.

"Oh, you managed to fix it," she said eagerly as she came toward them. A relieved smile lit her face. "That's wonderful. Now you can call a doctor and—"

"Sign off, Gunner." Jon's words cut through her sentence with the sharpness of a razor. "And then you'd better leave us alone."

"Great idea." Gunner turned back and spoke into the receiver. "We'll get back to you later, Barnett." He clicked off the unit, pushed back his chair, and stood up. "I'll go up and keep an eye on Andrew."

"He's sleeping," Elizabeth said, her gaze on Jon's face. His expression was more grim than she'd ever seen it. Her smile vanished. "What's wrong? What's happened, Jon?"

"Nothing has happened. Everything is exactly the same. It's just that the situation isn't what you thought it was."

Gunner paused beside her, his gaze warmly sympathetic. He murmured in an undertone, "Don't be too hard on him. He hated like hell to handle things this way. He didn't see any other solution." The door closed behind him.

"I don't understand," Elizabeth said haltingly. She tried to laugh. "I wish you'd explain, you're frightening me."

"I don't mean to frighten you. Damn, I hope you won't be frightened."

"Well, you're not succeeding. You're scaring the daylights out of me. Now *tell* me. Is it something you heard on the radio?"

He was silent for a moment. "The radio was never out of order," he finally said quietly. "The roads weren't closed more than a few hours during the entire time we've been here. There's nothing wrong with Andrew. His appetite is flourishing, according to Gunner."

"According to Gunner," she repeated dazedly. She was trying to comprehend something, anything, and clutched desperately at the last fact he had thrown out at her.

"Gunner's taken over Andrew's night and afternoon feedings. He's been bottle-feeding him before bringing him to you for the last week. I decided it was necessary for both your sakes that he be gradually switched to bottled formula."

"*You* decided." She stared at him in disbelief. "What right have you to make decisions concerning my son?" A smoldering anger began to simmer inside her. "Dammit, what right?"

"I took the right."

"I can't believe it. I can't believe any of this. You lied to me."

"Yes."

She shook her head in confusion. "From the beginning, everything has been a lie."

A flicker of pain crossed his face. "Not everything. I love you. I'll do everything in my power to watch over you and protect you. I wasn't lying about that."

"How can I believe you? How can I believe anything you do or say? You not only lied to me, you robbed me of something very important. You knew how I felt about breast-feeding Andrew. And that's the craziest thing of all. What possible reason could you have for doing that?"

"There may be periods when you and Andrew will have to be separated to ensure your safety. It wasn't practical for you to continue to breast-feed. I gave you as long as I could."

"Gave me?" Her eyes were blazing. "How tolerant! I've never met anyone so arrogant in my life. No one gives me permission to care for my son. I'll do as I see fit." Her hands clenched into fists at her sides. "And now I'm wondering how many more lies you've told me. I'm wondering about the charming Mr. Bardot. Was he the real thing or another lie to panic me into running into your arms?" She laughed harshly. "And I did run into your arms, didn't I? I was so grateful for your kindness. So *damn* grateful."

"Bardot is the genuine article. I wish to hell he wasn't. He's been causing us a great many problems. I would have waited until the child was born before I approached you, if he hadn't been on the scene." Jon's lips twisted. "As long as the birth was simple and uncomplicated, we could risk it. We didn't want to isolate you like this."

"Then why did you? Why did you force me to have my child here instead of in a hospital? Why did you make me a prisoner? Why did you lie and cheat?"

He flinched. "Because you would have been too vulnerable, dammit. Bardot isn't fool enough to neglect having the hospitals watched." He paused. "And if there had been complications, the hospital might have run tests on Andrew. We couldn't permit that to happen. They might have discovered there were certain . . . differences."

She turned pale with fear. "What do you mean? There's nothing wrong with Andrew. He's healthy, you said so yourself."

"No, nothing's wrong. He's far healthier than you could possibly realize. That wasn't the difference I was referring to. There are bound to be certain anomalies in his brain waves considering that Mark was his father."

"Brain waves. Why should the fact Mark was his father have anything to do—" She broke off. "Mark didn't have a brain tumor or anything, did he?"

"No, but he wasn't like other men." Jon's voice

was very gentle. "He had an expanded mental capacity, Beth. If he had lived another ten years he would have far surpassed Einstein in intelligence. Given another twenty years there would have been no limit, no comparison to any intelligence known."

She stared at him in shock. "You're insane," she whispered. "Mark was intelligent, but there was nothing unusual about him."

"I suppose I should have expected you to react this way. I assure you, I'm not even a little unbalanced. My genetic structure completely rules out any possibility of a mental disorder, according to the Clanad's genetic committee. Unfortunately, I have a few other genetic qualities they find less admirable."

"Clanad?" she asked faintly.

"The group to which Mark belonged." He paused. "The group to which Gunner and I also belong."

"You're claiming Mark was some sort of . . . superbrain? How would that make him a danger to anyone?"

"He *wouldn't* have been a danger, but men like Bardot refuse to believe that. They equate being different with being a threat. And, because Mark was a Garvanian, they automatically assumed that threat was directed against the United States."

"Mark wasn't American?"

Jon shook his head. "No, none of us are. We were all born in Garvania." His lips twisted. "I guess you could call us illegal aliens. We came here when we escaped from an institute in Said Ababa two years ago. It seemed the safest place for us to hide out and take stock of our situation. We didn't count on the NIB picking up our trail quite so quickly."

Elizabeth rubbed her temple dazedly. "I've never even heard of the existence of a country called Garvania."

"Not many people have heard of it. It was a tiny country lying between Said Ababa and Tamrovia." His tone became bitter. "You notice I use the past tense. Right after Said Ababa's revolution, the military decided to 'annex' Garvania. During all the turmoil, the invasion was scarcely noticed by anyone outside of our country. We definitely noticed, however. Those bastards made damn sure we did. They knew just what they wanted when they marched into Garvania and, when they found they couldn't get it, they decided to take the Clanad back to Said Ababa instead."

"What did they want?"

"Mirandite. It was a chemical substance found in certain plants in the Samarian jungle. The Garvanian scientists had discovered its properties five years before and were experimenting with a group of volunteers at the time of the invasion. The plant was extremely rare, and the substance almost impossible to extract even in minute quantities. The invaders were most annoyed to find the plant extinct by the time they arrived on the scene. However, they were delighted to learn the effect the chemical had on the volunteers was a permanent one."

She was shaking so badly, she could scarcely stand. As she turned blindly toward the door, she said, "I don't know what you think you've accomplished by telling me this wild tale. Maybe I was pretty gullible to believe all your other lies, but I'm not stupid."

His hand was on her shoulder, and he whirled her around to face him. "You *will* listen. Do you think this is easy for me? The only thing keeping me going is knowing I won't have to tell you any more lies. I hated that. You're going to hear it all. You may not believe me, but you won't be able to accuse me of not being honest with you." His other hand gripped her shoulder and he looked directly into her eyes. "The substance caused certain changes which enabled us to make an enormous breakthrough. You know that humans use only ten percent of their brains. Well, Mirandite permitted access to an additional thirty percent, perhaps more. Only time will tell. Not only was it effective, but it caused no cellular damage. However, it did alter our DNA, that is, it created genetic changes. The military junta in Said Ababa had dreams of increasing their own intelligence potential, but when they realized that was out of the question, they decided to see if they could make use of the Clanad. They treated us like animals, putting us through stress tests that almost destroyed us." He drew a shuddering breath. "After three years we managed to escape and come to the United States. There are fifty-three of us in the Clanad now that Mark is dead."

Elizabeth struggled wildly to free herself. Her mind was a chaos of pain, confusion, and rejection. "Let me go."

"In a moment. There's not much more to tell you. Mark left the group when he met and married you. There was nothing wrong with his leaving in the eyes of the Clanad. However, since there was a chance you might conceive a child, our genetic research committee did a thorough study on you. There were reasons why it was essential you have no hint of instability in your makeup. Our report on you was completely reassuring to us."

"How nice," Elizabeth said caustically.

"I know it sounds arrogant, but you'd understand if—" He stopped. "Look, I'm not saying there's anything special about us. We're like everyone else. It's just that we have the potential for more. When you became pregnant, Mark knew you'd need protection and resumed contact with us."

"Have you finished? May I go now?"

"No, you haven't heard about Andrew."

She stiffened. "What about Andrew?"

"He's the first child born of a member of the Clanad and an outsider."

"And?"

"We have reason to believe the mind expansion capability can be inherited. It's only a chance, but our scientists think it's a promising one. If what they believe is true, it means we'd no longer be an elite group and, in time, the ability could spread throughout the general population. Dear God, how we want that to happen."

She laughed. "You're saying Andrew is some kind of superbaby, and I'm just a glorified brood mare? Your story becomes wilder by the moment. You can't expect me to believe you."

"Not right now." He drew an uneven breath. "But you'll come to believe me in time, because I give you my promise, every word is true. I'll never lie to you again, Beth."

"It's too late. How can I ever trust you?" She closed her eyes. "Just listen to me. I'm talking to you as if you were a rational human being."

"I am rational and very, very human."

Her lids lifted to reveal eyes brimming with tears. "Please don't go on. I don't think I can take anymore."

He released her shoulders and stepped back. "All right. I'll give you some breathing space, but you're not going to get away from me. We belong together."

Her laugh was almost a sob. "Your precious committee told you so?"

"Yes, and I knew it myself the minute they showed me the video tapes of you." He went on calmly, "I don't always agree with genetic pairing, but in our case it couldn't be more right."

"Please. It *hurts*, dammit." She turned to the door. "I'd rather you told me nothing than to listen to you make up fairy tales. I trusted you. I think I even—" She broke off. She couldn't speak without weeping, and she would not cry. She tore open the door, and ran up the stairs. Crazy. Everything was topsy-turvy, and there was nothing good and true to hold onto in the entire world.

She had to return to reality. She had to return to Andrew. Yet, according to Jon, Andrew was the center of the madness. No, she wouldn't believe it. Andrew was her son, Mark's son. Dear, and beautiful, and infinitely sweet. She felt a strong impulse to look at him, hold him, reassure herself that Jon's words were pure fabrication.

When she opened the door of Andrew's nursery, she saw Gunner sitting in the chair across from

Andrew's makeshift crib, with her son cradled in his arms. It always amazed her how completely at ease Gunner looked holding the infant. Virile, tough, and totally masculine, he still handled her baby with the gentleness and instinctive understanding of a loving and skillful nursemaid. He looked up now, a sunny smile on his face. "Hi. He began to cry, so I rocked him to back to sleep. Once we're settled we're going to have to get a superdeluxe rocking chair." He stood up and carried the baby back to his crib.

She stood looking at him helplessly. It seemed impossible that Gunner also had deceived her. He was her friend. Over the last weeks she had become closer to him than anyone she had ever known except Mark and Jon.

He settled Andrew back in his crib, and Elizabeth found the tenderness in his action poignantly moving. "You know, babies have such wonderfully simple minds. They feel hunger, love, anger. No complications. I guess that's why I enjoy them so much." He didn't take his gaze from Andrew's face. "Are you very upset?"

"Yes."

"He told you everything?"

"He told me a bunch of convoluted fairy tales."

"Then he told you everything. I suppose you're angry with us?"

"You had no business . . ." Oh, what was the use, she thought. "You're damn right I'm angry."

He raised his eyes to look at her gravely. "When you get over your first bout of anger, you might consider how hard it was for Jon to play out this charade. Jon is the head of the Clanad and he could have sent anyone to care for you and Andrew. He wields more power than you can possibly imagine. He chose to come himself." He added simply, "He chose you."

"Not you too," Elizabeth said wearily. "This insanity must be contagious." She crossed to the chest on the other side of the room and opened the top drawer. "Well, I'm not going to let either one of you infect my son." She took out two small woolen squares that Gunner had cut from a full-size blanket and tossed them on a chair. "Andrew and I will be saying adieu to your Mad Hatter's Tea Party. And I wouldn't try to stop me, if I were you."

"It's not my place to make any decisions regarding you and Andrew. That's strictly Jon's prerogative. He's been very patient. But don't try his patience too far, Elizabeth. The genes that make him a brilliant leader also give him a very short fuse."

"I'm getting very tired of all this talk about genes," Elizabeth said curtly. "And my own fuse is nonexistent at the moment. Tell Jon to have the pickup truck in front of the lodge in fifteen minutes. I want it warmed up and ready to go. I won't have Andrew exposed to the cold."

"Yes, ma'am." His lips twitched. "Though I can't vouch for Jon's reaction to your command. I don't believe anyone has ever asked him to be a parking valet before. Remind me to tell you about the province he ruled in Garvania sometime."

"I'm not in the mood for your fables, Gunner. However, I'm definitely in the mood for a good old-fashioned rhubarb. If the truck's not ready when I come downstairs, that's exactly what the two of you are going to get." Her gaze was flint hard. "Understand?"

"I understand." He saluted and turned toward the door with a smile of amusement. "I only hope I can make Jon understand."

When Elizabeth came out on the deck twenty minutes later, the truck was waiting.

The exhaust tossed clouds of vapor into the cold air, and Jon stood by the cab with his hands in the pockets of his coat. His face was completely expressionless as he met her gaze. "The gas tank is full. You shouldn't have to stop."

"That's good." Why was she feeling so guilty? she wondered. She was the one who had been deceived, who was still being deceived, yet she felt as if she were deserting them.

Gunner jumped down from the cab of the truck. "I've installed an infant restraint seat," he said as he climbed the steps toward her. "You'll find his clothes and disposable diapers behind the front seat."

"So much for improvisation. You were obviously prepared all along." Her flash of anger at this new evidence of deceit banished the irrational guilt she'd felt. "It must have annoyed you to have to plan all those elaborate makeshift arrangements for Andrew, just to pull the wool over my eyes."

Gunner's golden hair shimmered in the late afternoon sunlight as he shook his head. "I didn't mind. It was kind of a challenge." He took Andrew from her. "I'll get Andrew settled comfortably in the infant seat for you."

As he walked quickly toward the truck, she stared after him in helpless frustration. How could she remain angry when Gunner was so damnably helpful and understanding?

"Nothing has really changed, you know," Jon said quietly, his gaze fixed shrewdly on her face. "The basic facts remain the same. Gunner and I both still love you and Andrew. We're still the same men you've lived with for the past month and a half. The same men you called your family the night Andrew was born. Try to remember that, when you think about all this."

"Everything's changed." She tore her gaze away from his and hurried down the steps. She had to get away. She had to escape from all the confusion and hurt and . . . "Everything."

He opened the door on the driver's side of the truck. "There's one other thing you should remember. You mustn't ever doubt the love Mark felt for you." His words were halting. "Andrew was conceived in love, Beth." He reached into his pocket and handed her an envelope. "It's a note from Mark. If I were you, I'd wait to read it until I could think a little more lucidly."

She slipped the note into her pocket without looking at it. Her throat was tight and her vision blurred. No, she mustn't be swayed by him. "Goodbye, Jon." She stepped up into the cab of the truck.

Gunner got out of the passenger seat, and gestured toward Andrew as he lay esconced in the luxuriously padded restraint seat. "He should be comfortable. Check the straps later to be sure they don't loosen." He waved cheerfully as he shut the door.

Jon took a step nearer, his black eyes blazing fiercely in his pale face. "Mark loved you, but he didn't love you as much as I do. No one could love you the way I do. Remember that, too, dammit." He stepped back and slammed the door of the truck. "And for heaven's sake, drive carefully."

Gunner crossed to stand beside Jon. She started the ignition and began to drive slowly down the driveway toward the road.

"You know she's driving right into Bardot's trap," Gunner murmured. "I'm surprised you let her go."

"I had to let her go." Jon's gaze never left the pickup truck. "She was practically shellshocked. She needed to run away and hide until she could come to terms with everything. She needed to go . . . home."

"Bardot won't let her hide away for long. He's bound to have the cottage under surveillance."

"It may be long enough." Jon turned away and began to climb the steps of the deck. "We've taken a hell of a lot away from her. We owe her this. Come on, we've got to alert Barnett so he can put a watch on Bardot's headquarters. I have to know when he makes his move. Then we'll have to close up the lodge and get on the road ourselves. I don't want to be more than an hour behind her."

Seven

Elizabeth drove past the white barn that had the feed advertisement on its sloped roof.

Home. Soon. The Burma Shave signs no longer lined the road, but the familiar red silo was still visible just ahead. Thank heavens some things stayed the same, she thought. How she needed to feel a sense of continuity and tranquillity now. After she drove past the silo, and rumbled over the covered bridge, the cottage came into view.

Andrew stirred in the restraint chair, and she cast him a quick glance. She knew he had been awake for the entire journey and was pleased at how good he'd been. "It's all right, love. We're almost home."

She spoke the comforting words as much for herself as for Andrew. Everything would be fine; the pain would go away and sanity would return. All she needed was to spend time in familiar sur-

roundings. Time had dulled her pain after her
mother and father had died, it had soothed her
when she had lost Mark. Surely time would work
the same magic on the raw agony she was experiencing now. Jon was virtually a stranger to her
after all. She should be able to forget she had
almost fallen in love with him.

Almost. No, she wouldn't lie to herself. She had
loved Jon Sandell. Why else would she be going
through hellish agony at the realization that he
had been using her for his own purposes? Lies.
So many lies and a preposterous story . . .

She pulled into the driveway in front of the
cottage, and sighed with relief. She turned off the
ignition and unstrapped Andrew from the infant
seat. Home.

Forty-five minutes later Andrew was freshly diapered, fed, and comfortably settled for his nap on
her big bed.

She was sorry she had completed the small tasks.
When she was busy, she didn't have time to think.
Now she had nothing to do, and she was as confused as she'd been on the long drive home from the
lodge.

She wandered to the window and looked down
at the stream below. The water wasn't frozen yet,
but it looked icy and cold under the iron-gray sky.
She shivered. Her entire world was cold now. Only
a few hours before she had been surrounded by
warmth and love and . . . No, it had been a lie.

She reached toward the switch on the wall that
activated the paddle wheel and turned it on. The
old oak wheel shuddered at first, and then began
to turn slowly, shedding its blanket of snow as it

dipped into the cold water of the stream. How Mark had loved to hear the sound of the paddles hitting the water. Mark. The letter.

She turned away from the window and picked up her navy coat which she had tossed on the rocking chair when she had walked into the room. Was the letter really from Mark, or had Jon lied about that too? she wondered. She pulled the letter out from the pocket of her coat. Her name was written in Mark's familiar, precise script on the front of the envelope.

Oh, Lord, Mark! It was Mark's handwriting. Unmistakably Mark's. She felt tears sting her eyes. Her hands shook as she took the single sheet of paper from the envelope. The letter was very short, hardly more than a note.

My Darling,

It's all very bewildering, isn't it? I wish I could be with you to help you understand. There were many times when I was tempted to tell you the truth, minutes when I held you in my arms and told myself it would be better if you heard it from me. But I found I was too selfish to say the words. I knew I'd have you for only a few months, and I wanted those months to be perfect. So I left it to Jon to tell you the truth, and I continued to enjoy my perfect months together with you.

And they were perfect, Elizabeth. You gave me everything I'd ever wanted in a woman. I can't tell you how wonderful I found our

time together at Mill Cottage after the hell
I'd been through in Said Ababa.

The burden I left Jon with was a heavy
one, and I hope to make it up to him by
adding my assurances to his. It's true, Elizabeth. Garvania, the Clanad, it's all true.

It's also true that I love you and will love
you until the moment of my death. Thank
you for giving me your love and letting me
share your life.

Goodbye,
Mark

Elizabeth could feel the tears running slowly
down her cheeks. Reading his poignant note
was almost as painful as losing him a second
time. Yet now the pain was partially diluted by
shock.

Mark was the person whose integrity she had
trusted most in the world and he had said Jon's
wild story was absolutely factual. If her judg-
ment of Mark was a true one, then she must
believe what he told her was also true. But how
could a sane person believe a story that was
similar to the plot of a Steven Spielberg movie?

She sank down into the rocking chair, Mark's
letter still clutched in her hand. Her mind was
whirling, but she had to think. She had to
try to sift out the truth from the fable. Her
gaze fastened on the slow turning of the paddle
wheel outside the window. The steady, deliberate
rhythm soothed her as it always did, and she
settled back in the chair and leaned her head

on its cushioned headrest. Love. Lies. Truth. Fantasy.

For centuries her forbears had steeped themselves in healthy Yankee pragmatism, but they'd still left ample room for vision. She was a Cartwright. She possessed the same qualities herself. She had the strength to accept or reject what she chose to believe as truth. She would sit here, and decide what she was going to do.

"Beth."

He said her name softly, the sound floating into the dusk-shrouded room as gently as a shadow. Jon. She didn't turn around, but kept her gaze on the paddle wheel. His presence there was no surprise to her. She had expected him to come. She knew he had to come.

"Beth, we have to leave. I've received word Bardot has left the farm and will be at the cottage within the hour. It's not safe here any longer." He came forward to stand beside the rocking chair.

"Hello, Jon." Her voice was quiet, almost casual.

"Beth, I know you haven't had much time but—"

"I've had time enough. Sit down, Jon. I want to ask you a question."

"Later. I have to get you and Andrew out of here."

"Now." Her tone was edged with steel. "I'm not going to put you through an interrogation, but there's one thing I have to know."

He sat down on the cushioned window seat opposite her. The dimness of the room prevented her from seeing the expression on his face, but she sensed his impatience by the charged tension in his body. "What is it?"

"In Mark's letter he said he knew he would have only a few months with me. What did he mean?"

Jon didn't answer for a long moment. "Mark had a heart ailment that was aggravated by the ordeal we went through in Said Ababa. If he hadn't been killed in the accident, he would have died within a short time anyway. That was why he left the Clanad. The doctors told him he had only six months to live, and he wanted something we couldn't give him. He wanted to live a normal life."

"Oh, no." Elizabeth closed her eyes. Golden, beautiful Mark. Her Mark.

"A martyr." There was a thread of pain in Jon's voice. "Not only perfect, but a bloody martyr. How can a man compete with that?"

"You didn't have to tell me."

"Yes, I did. He deserved to have you know. He was everything you thought he was. He was good, kind, and brave. I may be jealous as hell, but I won't cheat him of his due."

"Thank you," she whispered.

The only sound in the room came from the creaking of the paddle wheel outside.

"You believe me now?"

Her eyes opened. "I believe Mark. It's going to take a long time before I can believe you again."

They were both silent.

"I guess I'm going to have to accept that fact." He paused. "For the moment. Can we leave now?"

"Not yet. I must talk to Bardot." She raised her hand as he started to protest. "I have to do it. It's one thing to accept impossibilities on a remote level of consciousness, but it has to become *real* to me. There's too much at stake. I'm too tired now to comprehend all the ramifications."

"If you won't leave yourself, will you at least allow me to take Andrew? Gunner is waiting downstairs and can get the baby away from here before Bardot arrives. You know you can trust Gunner to take good care of Andrew."

Yes, she could trust Gunner, but could she bear to part with Andrew? Of course she could. She had no right to put her son in danger because she needed more assurance. "All right." She rose to her feet and went over to the bed where Andrew still slept peacefully. "Gunner can take Andrew. I'll bring him downstairs right away."

"Good." Jon stood up and turned toward the door. "I'll go give Gunner instructions about our rendezvous later."

Five minutes later when Elizabeth came downstairs, Jon and Gunner were waiting in the foyer.

"Hi, I hear Andrew and I are going to have a chance to finish our book." Gunner smiled as he took Andrew's blanket-swathed body from her. "I had a hunch we would. I just happen to have brought old Einstein with me."

"That's wonderful." Her hands lingered as she tucked the blanket more securely about her son.

Heavens, she didn't want to let him go. "Keep him safe, Gunner."

"I will."

"Someone may try to stop you when they see you leave the cottage with Andrew. There may even be a roadblock." Jon met Gunner's gaze steadily. "Don't risk defending him by the usual means. While Andrew is in your custody, you have permission to ignore the raznal."

Gunner's eyes widened in shock. Then he gave a low whistle of delight and appreciation. "I was wondering if you'd lift the ban. It won't be as much fun, but I guess it will be safer for Andrew. I'll see you later when we rendezvous." He turned away, his arms tightening around the baby. "Come on, kid. Let's go get 'em."

Elizabeth watched as Gunner got into the truck and strapped Andrew into his car seat. "He will be safe, won't he?"

"Perfectly safe," Jon said. "I wouldn't have let Gunner take him if I hadn't been sure of his safety."

"What does raznal mean?"

Jon hesitated. "It's something like a taboo, only infinitely stronger."

"What kind of taboo?"

"I'll explain later." Jon's lips twisted in a crooked smile. "I think you've had enough to absorb for the time being."

Gunner started to back the truck out of the driveway, and she turned away with a weary sigh. "Perhaps you're right, I do seem to have an overabundance of facts on my mind at the moment. But that doesn't mean you're going to get away with dribbling bits of information to me as you see fit. There are a hell of a lot of questions I need answered, and you're going to supply the answers."

"I have no objections." He closed the door. "I want to answer your questions. It will be a relief. Once everything is out in the open, maybe you'll be able to trust me again."

"Perhaps."

He flinched, and she felt a sharp twinge of remorse beneath the numbness she was experiencing. Is this what emotional burnout felt like? She had gone through so much upheaval that she couldn't feel anything anymore.

The pain in his expression was quickly shuttered. "Well, shall we go into the sitting room and wait for Bardot? He should show up within the next ten minutes."

She shook her head. "I'll wait in the sitting room, you go upstairs and wait in my bedroom. I'll join you as soon as I've finished with Bardot."

He frowned. "The hell I will. I'm not leaving you alone with that bastard."

"You have no choice. This is my home and I'm going to face Bardot alone." She gazed at him, her eyes blazing. "I won't allow you to interfere any longer, Jon. I was catapulted into this situation without being asked, but now that I'm in it, I refuse to act like a puppet. I'll never be manipulated by you again."

He stood glaring at her. "Dammit, why the hell are you so stubborn? I only want to do what's best for you."

"Stubbornness is an old, revered Yankee characteristic, and so is independence. You ought to appreciate those qualities in my genetic makeup."

She smiled sadly. "You Garvanians seem very hung up on that kind of thing. Now leave me alone. Stay out of my battles unless you receive an invitation."

"Beth . . ." He stood looking at her in frustration and anger. Then he whirled around and headed for the stairs barely able to control his violent emotions. "All right, fight your own battles. I'll be upstairs with the door open. If I hear even a loud word, I'm coming back down."

"I don't suppose you have a gun?"

He looked at her in surprise. "Would you use it, if I did?"

"I don't know. I once thought I could never tolerate the idea of hurting another human being. Now . . . Andrew . . ." Her expression reflected both her bewilderment and sadness. "I just don't know."

"I don't have a gun, Elizabeth. We don't need guns," Jon said gently. "Someday I hope no one will." He began climbing the stairs. "Don't let Bardot give you too much flack before you bring your meeting to an end."

"Come in, Mr. Bardot. I've been waiting for you." Elizabeth glanced at the two men who flanked Bardot. "The invitation doesn't include your friends. Tell them to wait in the car."

"You're damn cocky for a woman in such a vulnerable position," Karl Bardot said with a growl. He looked over his shoulder, and spoke to his assistants. "Go wait in the car. You'll get to know the lady soon enough." He smiled unpleasantly. "In fact, you'll practically be roommates."

The shorter of the two men snickered, and then he and his cohort sauntered back to the sedan parked in the driveway.

"Satisfied?" Bardot drawled.

Elizabeth nodded as she stepped aside so he could enter. "No amenities this time, Mr. Bardot." She shut the door and leaned back against it. "I'll be very frank. I let you in for only one reason. I want answers."

"You let me in because you knew you couldn't keep me out. And I let you have your moment of power, because I want an answer too. What happened to my men?"

"Your men?"

"Don't play innocent with me. I'm talking about the men I had watching this house. They radioed me that they had seen a man leave the cottage carrying a baby. I ordered them to intercept and capture him."

Elizabeth felt the breath leave her body. "And?"

Bardot's jowls firmed as he gritted his teeth. "Where are they, dammit? That was the last transmission we had from them. We can't reach them on the radio, and there was no sign of anyone on the road. What have you done with them?"

"I have no idea." She was almost faint with relief. Andrew and Gunner were safe. How in the world had Gunner managed it? She wondered.

"The hell you don't. You came back here bold as brass with your brat in tow—"

"If you're speaking about my son, please show a little respect. I dislike hearing him referred to as a brat." She smiled coolly. "And why shouldn't I come back? This is my home."

"Not for long. Not after I prove what you are."

"And what am I, Mr. Bardot?"

"An accessory to the plot."

"What plot?"

"The plot to take us over."

Elizabeth drew a deep, shaky breath. She had wanted the situation to become real to her, and she was certainly getting her wish. Nothing could be more real than the pale blue eyes that were glaring venomously into her own.

"You spoke of an autopsy report on my husband. Proof of his uniqueness. What did you mean by that?"

He laughed harshly. "You know what I meant. You know what the report said."

"Do I? Why don't you tell me?"

"Your husband wasn't like us. He was a freak."

"You're saying he had physical abnormalities?"

"I'm saying he was a damn freak. There were actual alterations to the cells of his brain."

"Perhaps the report was in error."

"That's what you want us to believe. That's why you had Ramsey's body cremated so quickly after the autopsy. The report wasn't in error, but you didn't want us to be able to double check the findings, much less to have physical evidence. We've been aware for years what those creeps in Said Ababa have been up to. We even knew when they began to infiltrate us."

"I don't believe you. Even if Mark was what you say he was, why would you try to persecute him? Why wouldn't you welcome him?"

Bardot stared at her as if he were dumbfounded. "He was the enemy. He was different. If he'd meant to do good by us, why didn't he march right up and knock on the White House door, instead of sneaking around under cover?"

"Perhaps because he realized the world has a great many Karl Bardots," she said wearily.

"That's what I'd expect from a slut who'd marry a freak like Ramsey."

She straightened. "Mark was *not* a freak. He was everything kind and . . ." She stopped. It was no use. Bardot's mind was closed too tightly to yield to either truth or reason. "I believe we've said all there is to say. Please leave."

His lips curled. "Not this time. You're coming with me. Do I have to call my men or are you going to come peacefully?"

Elizabeth had been expecting this reaction. "Since you put it that way, I'll have to come. You offered to let me pack a suitcase the last time. Is the offer still good?"

He looked surprised and a little uneasy at her swift acquiescence. "I guess that would be all right." He crossed the few feet to the front door. "But don't think you have a chance of escaping. I have men at both the front and back doors. I'll give you ten minutes, and then we're coming in after you."

Elizabeth held her breath until the front door closed behind him. Ten minutes. Only ten minutes. She ran to the front door and slid the safety bolt shut. Then she ran up the stairs, taking them two at a time.

Jon was at the bedroom door before she reached it. "Well, is it real enough for you now?"

"Yes." Elizabeth ran to the window seat, kneeled and threw open the casement windows. "It couldn't be more real, and I'll be damned if I'll let that idiot get his hands on you or Andrew or Gunner."

He smiled. "I'm glad Gunner and I are on your protected list. However, I might remind you he doesn't realize who Gunner and I are yet. You're the one who is in danger."

"From what Bardot told me, he may know more than you think he does," she said. "How long do you think it would take him to find out you're one of the Clanad after he captured you?"

"That's a good point." He was frowning as he watched her pull off her boots. "May I ask what in the world you're doing?"

"We have to get out of here. You'd better leave your coat. It will only weigh you down in the water. Hurry!"

He automatically shrugged out of his jacket. "I assume we're going for a swim. How are we going to get to the stream? It's a two-story drop and someone's bound to hear the splash if we dive."

"We're not going to dive. We're going to ride the paddles of the wheel down."

"The paddles?" He suddenly began to chuckle. "Now I truly believe the committee's report on you, Elizabeth Cartwright Ramsey. Strength and initiative, they said." His eyes danced with amusement. "I'd say your plan demonstrates that they hit it right on the genetic bull's-eye."

"Genes, again?" she asked tartly. "Here we call it good old Yankee know-how." She balanced on the window seat. "Follow me."

"Beth, we don't have to do this. It's not necessary. I can—" He broke off.

She glanced at him over her shoulder. "What?"

He gazed at her silently for a moment, as a series of emotions showed on his face. "Nothing." He smiled curiously. "Nothing at all. I'll be glad to follow you." He kicked off his boots and crossed the room in his stockinged feet. "Anywhere. Lead on, my dear Yankee."

Eight

"Put your feet on a paddle first, and then as the wheel goes down, grab another paddle with your hands and hold on for dear life." She scooted to the edge of the windowsill. "You have to hop a little to mount the wheel."

"Your expertise in this area is truly amazing."

"I grew up in this house. Do you think that as a child I could have resisted the temptation to play on a real oak paddle wheel? Every summer I would—" She jumped and landed on a paddle, immediately grabbing onto another, which was at eye level. The wood was wet and slippery beneath her palms. "Hurry," she whispered.

The paddle creaked beneath her weight but held firm. She felt the wheel jerk as Jon landed on a paddle somewhere above her.

The wind cut through the bulky wool of her thigh-length sweater. Cold. So cold. But not as cold as it was going to be. The still waters of the stream were just below her, coming closer every second as the wheel slowly rotated.

Finally the paddle she was riding entered the water.

She inhaled sharply as the icy water took her breath away and sent stabbing icicles of shock through her veins. She released the paddle and started to swim as quietly as she could away from the cottage. Her every movement was labored, as she forced her numbed arms to cleave through the water.

"All right?" Jon whispered. He was beside her now.

"Yes." Her answer was slurred. "But I think we'd better get out of the water as soon as we can. It's dangerous to be immersed in temperatures this cold for too long. Do you think we're out of sight? I wanted to get to the woods but . . ."

"Hush. Don't try to talk." His arm was around her waist as he headed for the bank. "Lean on me. I'll have you out of this water in a minute."

His movements were strong as he swam easily through the water. The cold didn't seem to be affecting him at all, she thought hazily. How could that be? He should be feeling the extremely low temperature of the water more acutely than she. He had said his country was warmer. . . .

He released her, hoisted himself up on the bank, and then pulled her up alongside him.

Her teeth were chattering uncontrollably as she tried to wring some of the water from the bottom of her sweater. Her gaze flew to the cottage. It was so close. Too close. They were barely halfway across the meadow. She shrugged out from under Jon's arm and jumped to her feet. "We've got to get to the woods. I know a place. We're too close here. They'll be breaking into the cottage any minute."

"Beth, you can't go on. The cold—" His tone was thick with self-disgust. "Lord, I'm stupid. I thought I saw a way to clear my path and forgot you weren't . . ."

She wasn't listening. She was running across the snow-covered meadow toward the woods.

Twigs and stones lying under the blanket of snow tore at her sodden socks, but at least she could feel the blood pumping through her veins again. If only the wind would stop plastering her damp clothes to her body, she might even feel warm. Where was Jon? she wondered. They mustn't catch him. It would be worse for him to be captured than for her. "Jon." She looked over her shoulder. He was right behind her, she realized with relief. "Are you okay?"

"Am I—" He drew a deep breath. "I'm fine. Where the hell is the haven you're taking me to? I hope it's warm."

"Are you very cold? You said you were from a desert country." Desert country, she repeated to herself. It sounded wonderful. The sun's hot rays baking the cold from her bones. "I don't think it will be very warm, but they won't be able to find us. At least, not until morning. There's a cave in the wall of the bluff where I used to play when I was a child. I fixed it all up. I'm looking forward to showing it to Andrew. It's right here." She leaned against the lichen-covered stone of the bluff, trying to catch her breath. "Will you roll the boulder away from the entrance? I can't seem to stop shivering." It was more than shivering, she was shuddering violently. "I don't know why I'm reacting this way. I'm much warmer now."

"Are you?" Jon's expression was grim as he rolled aside the heavy boulder. "Stay here for just a minute while I check your hideaway for foreign invaders."

"According to Bardot, you should feel right at home with them."

"Is there a flashlight inside?"

She shook her head. "No, but there's an oil lantern and a box of matches to the left of the entrance."

He was gone only a few minutes, and when he came back he was carrying the lantern. "Come inside. Your provisions don't seem to include anything to make a fire."

"I only came here during the summer. In the winter it was too cold. I think there are two patchwork quilts." She glanced around. "Yes, there they are. My mother helped me make the one that has the little girls wearing sunbonnets on it. I was only eight years old, and she said she was very proud of me."

"It's a beautiful quilt. Any mother would be proud," Jon said gently. "Now stay here while I roll the stone back into place. Okay?"

"Okay."

She watched him as he grappled with the enormous stone. The muscles of his back and shoulders rippled beneath the wet clinging material of his red plaid shirt. When the boulder was in place, he turned to face her.

"You're very wet. I'm sorry there's no firewood." She reached up to brush a wet lock of hair away from her cheek. "We could try to find some outside, but it would probably be useless. The snow . . . I hate winter. Did I tell you that?"

"Yes." He spread one of the quilts on the ground. "Come here, Beth."

"Are we going to try to sleep?" She came toward him as obediently as a small child.

"Yes." He pulled her sweater over her head and tossed it on the ground. "But first we're going to get you warm."

"I'm warm now. I don't know why I'm shaking like this."

"I do. A deadly little malady called hypothermia." His voice was suddenly savage. "And it's my fault, dammit. I should never have let you jump into that water. I could have . . ." The breath he drew sounded like a harsh rasp. "Look Beth, I have to get you warm. If I don't, you could go into shock and die. I know you said you couldn't trust me, but you don't have any choice." He unbuttoned her blouse and unfastened her bra.

"You've done this before. You're always undressing me."

"It appears that way, doesn't it? I'm glad it amuses you. I hope you still think it's funny when you're back to normal." He took off her wet jeans, panties, and socks.

"It doesn't seem logical to strip a person naked to get them warm."

Jon undressed, too, and joined her on the quilt. "It's very logical. We'll share body heat." He pulled the second quilt over both of them. "But that's not going to be enough. It's very cold here and you're already suffering from exposure. You'll have to let me help you. You mustn't fight me, Beth."

"Of course, it wouldn't be sensible to object when someone is trying to save you from freezing to death."

"Stop laughing." Jon's tone was serious. "This is important for you to understand. I can help your body make the adjustments it needs. The human anatomy is a wonderful defensive organism, but sometimes it needs to be told what to do." He cupped her cheeks in his hands and held her gaze with his own.

What wonderful eyes he had, she thought dreamily. Dark and brilliant and glowing with kinetic force.

"I will never trespass, nor invade your privacy but I *must* do this." His naked flesh was warm against her own and the heat he was emitting surrounded her. "Now I'm going to talk to you, and I want you to listen very carefully. Will you do that for me?"

"Yes."

"Good." He smiled. "Because soon you're going to be warm, as warm as I am, and your body is going to work very hard to keep you warm all through the night." His lips touched her forehead in a gossamer-light caress, as he spun a web of golden tenderness around her. "Close your eyes and relax." He drew her closer so that her cheek nestled in the hollow of his shoulder. "There's nothing to worry about. I'll see that you don't go to sleep until it's safe for you. Just listen to me."

Later, she wouldn't be able to remember the

words he'd spoken. The sound of his voice flowed over her, around her, lighting torches of warmth and understanding where none had been lit before. Painting pictures of sunlit meadows overflowing with flowers of exquisite beauty, beauty veiled in warm mists and the songs of summer. Everywhere she passed, the torches flamed with indescribable splendor and reached into every part of her, filling her with a rapture so intense she didn't think she could bear it. She wasn't aware when the shivering stopped or when the numbness was replaced by genuine warmth.

His voice vibrated beneath her ear and the sensation was soothing. No, he'd stopped speaking, she realized, but she could still hear him. How very curious. Oh, there was nothing to worry about, she told herself. Jon said she shouldn't worry. He was taking care of everything. She would just lie here and let his voice ignite the torches within her.

"Beth." She felt a strong vibration beneath her ear. "You can go to sleep now."

The golden webbing that had enveloped her was gone, and so was the disorientation she'd experienced earlier. She felt a pang of wild regret. Loneliness. She had never known such loneliness. "Jon . . ."

His lips were on her temple. "I know."

He did know. She could still feel his empathy and understanding. "The torches." Her voice was slurred as drowsiness claimed her. So beautiful. "Come back."

"I can't, love."

"Please." The word was spoken as a mere breath of a sound.

"Someday."

It was a promise, and Jon always kept his promises. She had discovered that fact about him, as well as many other wonderful things, during the past hour.

"Someday," she echoed as she nestled her cheek against his hard shoulder. But there was something nagging at her, something she couldn't remember. It was something about the way Jon had looked at her before he had begun to light the torches. "The baby."

"What?"

She didn't open her eyes. "The night Andrew was born. What was in the milk?"

He gently stroked her hair back from one temple. "Nothing."

She had guessed what his answer was going to be. "Then you shouldn't have made me drink it. I *hate* warm milk."

"I didn't think you were ready to accept my help without a placebo."

"I don't know, maybe you were right." She was far too drowsy to talk any longer. She just wanted to drift away on the wings of sleep, now that there were no more lovely, radiant torches to be lit. . . .

She still felt warm when she opened her eyes the next morning. The cave was almost in total darkness, and the only sign of dawn was a thin wavering line of gray around the boulder hiding the entrance. Her naked breasts were pressed against Jon's warm, solid chest, and with every breath he drew she could feel the thatch of springy hair which covered his upper torso rub against her. Was it pain, or the fiery tingle of desire that caused her nipples to distend as if in yearning invitation? She edged away in confusion. The tempo of his breathing altered and she realized he was awake.

"Beth?"

"Do you think we should leave? It must be dawn." Her voice was breathless.

"Yes."

She laughed shakily. "Yes, it must be dawn, or yes, we should try to leave?"

"Did I sound confused? I'm afraid my reasoning processes aren't working too well at the moment."

Elizabeth's mental capabilities weren't in any better shape than Jon's. She couldn't seem to concentrated on anything but the heat flowing from his naked body to hers. She felt if she reached out and touched him, she would burn her hand. The rhythm of his breathing changed, harshened. She was having trouble breathing at all. "Do you think they're still out there?"

"I have no idea, and at the moment I could care less. Beth . . ." He reached out and suddenly the blanket was around her waist. "Beth, I'm hurting. I think you are too. Let me love you." His fingers touched her breasts, and she inhaled sharply. "Poor love, so full, so beautiful. I wish I could see you." His palms gently held her breasts. "Let me help you, taste you. Let me come into you. Let me take what you need to give. I'll show you pleasures you never dreamed existed. There are ways I—"

"Torches." She didn't even know she had uttered the word until she felt him stiffen against her.

His hands fell away from her breasts. His breathing was heavy and labored. "No!" He rolled away from her and curled up into a fetal position. She could feel his pain and desire and frustration as a living force in the darkness. "No torches, dammit. Get your clothes on."

"What?" She was jarred from her sensual haze as if she'd once again been plunged into the icy waters of the stream.

He spoke rapidly, not looking at her. "I hung our clothes on the boulder by the opening. I figured the wind might dry them. They're probably a little damp but—"

"*Why*, Jon?"

He didn't pretend to misunderstand her. "Because it's not fair. Because what you're feeling now could be a hangover from what I did to you last night."

"You did nothing to me, only for me. It was telepathy, wasn't it?"

"Yes, combined with deep hypnosis." He stood up and walked toward the entrance. She wished the light wasn't dim so that she could see more of him than just a shadow. Her mind had been so hazy when he'd stripped during the night, that she hadn't even noticed his body. She had only a vague memory of tight buttocks and powerful thighs. "And you told me the group you belong to is just like the rest of us," she said lightly. "Just ordinary small-town folks."

"Naturally increased psychic abilities are a result of mind expansion." His tone was threaded with irony. "Needless to say, the institute was delighted, and we were immediately taught to use all our abilities. The bastards didn't realize they'd given us the key to the cage they'd put us in."

"All?"

He was dressing swiftly. "All. What I did for you last night was fairly simple. The monks of Tibet have been able to control their body temperatures and organic functions for centuries. Our psychic abilities were the principal reason we decided we had to escape from Said Ababa as soon as possible. We had no desire to turn into a colony of madmen."

"Madmen?" Elizabeth's eyes widened. "What do you mean?"

He crossed back to her. "Later." He dropped her clothes on the quilt. "I'm in no mood to discuss the topic at the moment. It's beginning to get light in here. I can see you, and I'm hurting already."

"Can't you stop it? The way you helped me last night?"

"It doesn't work. I've tried it." She could barely discern his bittersweet smile in the half-dark interior of the cave. "It seems you're the cross I have to bear."

"I don't want you to hurt." Elizabeth's voice was troubled as she slowly began to dress. The material of her clothing was damp and cold against her skin. "You didn't have to stop, you know."

"I know, but when I make love to you, I'm going to make sure it's me you want. I know how seductive mental joining can be. I was inside your mind, sharing your emotions." His tone was halting. "I tried to make it beautiful for you."

"You did."

"I can make it more beautiful. When we're together, I can make you feel my desire, my satisfaction, as well as your own. I can let you physically feel what I feel—" He stopped and laughed harshly. "Just listen to me. With one hand I'm letting you go, and with the other I'm pulling you back. I'm no Mark Ramsey, am I?"

"No." Jon would never be the lovable idealist Mark had been, but she knew now she didn't want him to be. Last night when they had joined, she had discovered a beauty within him that shone as brightly as any she had found in Mark. He possessed integrity, strength, and a rigid set of values. He was also aggressive, passionate, possessive, and stubborn to the point of bullheadedness. No, he wasn't like Mark any more than the dawn resembled the sunset, but both had their own inner beauty and their own place in the scheme of things. And she knew now that Jon's place was in her life, for as long as she lived. "No, you're not Mark."

He flinched as if she'd struck him.

"No, I didn't mean—"

"You don't have to qualify your statement, I know I have a long way to go." He turned around and began to roll the stone away from the entrance. "But I do think we jumped a few hurdles last night. Finish getting dressed. I'll do some reconnoitering and be right back."

They'd jumped more than a few hurdles, Elizabeth thought as she pulled on her damp socks.

They'd made a quantum leap toward a closeness she never imagined was possible. Love. She loved Jon Sandell. Freely, proudly, and with her whole heart.

She couldn't deny that she had had apprehensions, and constantly had made comparisons between Jon and Mark. She supposed it was natural for Jon to jump to conclusions. Well, she had time to show him there would be no qualifications in her love for him, and no future comparisons to Mark.

However, she would prefer to wait until they were in a trifle more glamorous setting to stage her demonstration. She seemed destined always to appear at her worst when she was with Jon. First, she had been pregnant and was bulky and unwieldy with Andrew, and now she looked straggly and as stringy-haired as a veritable scarecrow.

"There's no sign of Bardot's men in the woods," Jon said from the entrance of the cave. "They're probably watching the road and the cottage, but if we skirt around the bluff and through the woods, we should make it."

"Make it to where?" Elizabeth rose to her feet and quickly began to fold the quilts. "You have a destination in mind, I hope?"

"Serena Spaulding's cottage. She's your good friend, and the one time I met her, she impressed me as being someone who wasn't afraid to take chances."

"Oh, you know Serena, all right. She'd punch the devil in the nose and then sue him for damages to her bruised knuckles." Elizabeth frowned as she came to stand beside him outside the cave.

"But I don't want her bruising those knuckles on my behalf. Bardot can be a very nasty customer."

"The only chance I'll ask her to take is to lend us her car and give you some dry clothes," Jon said soothingly.

"Won't Bardot's men be watching her cottage? His investigations must have turned up the fact that she's my best friend."

"We'll find a way to get into her place unseen. I don't like involving her in this mess any more than you do, but we need transportation. We have to rendezvous with Gunner tomorrow morning in Rochester."

"That's over two hundred miles."

"Hence the need for wheels. I know you don't want your friend in danger, and I promise she'll be safe. Trust me."

The frown vanished and a smile lit her face. "I do."

He took half a step forward and then stopped. "Thank God." His words were as fervent as a prayer. "It's been one hell of a rocky road."

"The most interesting ones usually are," she said lightly. "And you have to admit I've had some Herculean obstacles to overcome. I just want to know one thing. You don't plan to pull any other surprises out of your hat, do you?"

He frowned thoughtfully. "I don't think so."

"Good." She grinned up at him. "You don't know how relieved I am. So far I've been able to assimilate information on foreign intrigue, hypnosis, and telepathy. Just don't throw anything else at me. Deal?"

Something flickered in his face. "Beth, I . . ." He stopped and then smiled back at her. "Deal."

"Why do I suspect that you have reservations?" she asked warily.

"Now who's practicing telepathy?" He took her arm and began propelling her along the rough trail that bordered the bluff. "Let's hurry. I want you to get some shoes. I hope Serena wears the same size."

Serena's shoes were all far too narrow, but after searching through her brother's closet, she managed to come up with some moccasins that fitted Elizabeth fairly well, once the toes were stuffed with tissue.

"Are you sure Dane won't mind?" Elizabeth asked. "Will you at least let me pay for them, Serena?"

Serena made a face as she turned away from the closet. "Don't be ridiculous. Dane never wore half these clothes anyway. They're all far too primitive for his sophisticated tastes. And you know how seldom Dane honors me with his presence these days."

Elizabeth nodded slowly. Charming as Dane Spaulding undoubtedly was, no one could call him stable or a homebody. "Where is he now?"

"Monte Carlo. Someone told him there was a song written about the man who broke the bank at Monte Carlo, and he's vowed to add a few new verses to the chorus." Serena pulled a suitcase out of the closet. "So much for the peaceful life.

I'll probably have to mortgage my home and fly to his rescue."

"You'd enjoy every minute of it. You're as much of a wanderer as he is. I never understood how the two of you could own this lovely cottage and spend so little time in it. Don't you miss having a sense of permanence in your life?"

"Home is just a place to come back to rest, and permanence is boring as hell." Serena's violet eyes twinkled. "We're not all like you, Elizabeth. For some of us, what's down the road is more important than the ivy-covered cottage beside it." She slung the suitcase on the bed and unfastened it. "How long are you going to be gone? Will you need evening clothes?"

"No, we'll only be gone a few days." Elizabeth smiled. "And jeans will be far more practical than sequins and beads. This is definitely not a jaunt to Monte Carlo."

"Well, sequins and beads can be very morale-raising on occasion. Take it from one who knows. Now go back downstairs and keep that luscious man company while I pack this bag. I don't want you hemming and hawing over everything I throw in it." Serena held up her hand as Elizabeth started to protest. "You are *not* imposing. I finished the last of my sketches for the spring show, bundled them up, and sent them off to New York last weekend. I'm bored as the devil, and your little intrigue has brightened my day considerably." She threw open the lid of the suitcase. "I don't suppose you'd like to tell me what this is all about? Dogs with gunshot wounds, grim-looking types knocking on my door in the middle of the night, and now you two appearing mysteriously in my kitchen at the break of dawn. You have to admit it's enough to pique a woman's curiosity."

Grim-looking types. "Someone was here last night?"

Serena nodded. "The same man who was here after you dropped Sam off last month. Pale blue eyes." She puffed out her cheeks. "And jowls."

"Bardot. What did you tell him?"

"The same thing I told him the last time. That I didn't give a damn who he was, and if he took a step inside my house I'd shoot his kneecaps off."

Elizabeth laughed. "I can see how that would discourage him. What would you have done if he'd called your bluff?"

Serena's eyes widened in surprise. "What bluff? I was already planning what to wear in court. Something white and innocent, I thought. Brunettes usually can pull off the Madonna look." She lifted a dark, beautifully arched eyebrow. "You're not going to confide in me?"

"I can't. It's not that I don't want to tell you." Elizabeth's expression was distressed. "There are other people involved."

"Don't get upset. I just thought I'd ask. I know you wouldn't do anything wrong, and what are friends for if not to shoot the kneecaps off nasty types like Bardot? Now shoo, I'll be down in a few minutes." She turned to the mahogany chest of drawers beside the closet. "Pack yourselves a lunch for the road. There are cold cuts and Brie cheese in the refrigerator."

"Serena, you know I'll never be able to thank you."

"Then don't try." Serena's smile lit her beautiful face with warmth. "It will be less awkward for both of us. Do I get to keep Sam for a few more days? I've gotten accustomed to having the rascal around the house. He's company when Dane's away."

Elizabeth nodded. "We'll pick him up as soon as we come home. There has to be some quick way of straightening out this mess."

"I hope so. I'm looking forward to seeing young Master Andrew in the flesh."

"He's perfect," Elizabeth said softly. "And absolutely wonderful."

"I'm sure he is." Serena smiled gently. "You couldn't have a baby that wasn't wonderful. Just remember you said I could be his godmother. I'm holding you to that promise, no matter what. I've done all kinds of research on the duties and privileges involved in being a godmother."

"Research? You and Jon will obviously get along splendidly. He's a great one for research too. If you're lucky, he might even decide to make you a stained-glass window for your living room."

"Stained glass?" Serena asked, puzzled.

"Never mind." Elizabeth turned to the door. "And you'll definitely be Andrew's godmother. I wouldn't think of asking anyone else."

Jon was sitting at the kitchen table nursing the cup of coffee Serena had given him before she had taken Elizabeth upstairs. He also had benefited from Dane's wardrobe and had changed into boots, a pair of jeans, and a pale blue oxford-cloth shirt that had made his skin appear even more golden in contrast. He glanced up when Elizabeth walked into the room. "Okay?"

She nodded. "Serena is literally giving us the shirt off her back, and she'd probably sign the car over to us if we let her."

"I thought she would." He took a sip of coffee. "You're right, she's exceptionally attractive. She reminds me of Elizabeth Taylor in her younger days. She looks more like a model than a dress designer. Is she successful?"

"Fantastically so. If Serena were willing to settle down she could have her own fashion house, but she says it's too much responsibility and prefers to work for someone else. She was the designer who created the harem fashion fad last season." She suddenly frowned. "Bardot was here last night. Are you sure he won't cause Serena any trouble? What if he's watching the cottage when we drive off?"

"We're not going to drive off. We'll hike a few miles through the woods and then cut over to the road. Serena can meet us with the car and then walk back to the cottage."

"What if Bardot finds out she helped us?"

"He'll be so busy trying to locate us, he won't have time to harass her. Don't worry, I'll call and have a man sent to watch out for her as soon as we leave for Rochester."

Her eyes widened. "There are other Garvanians in the area? I don't know why, but I just assumed you and Gunner were the only ones."

He shook his head. "Andrew is very important to us. The moment we realized you were pregnant, we formed a network to protect him."

"He's very important to me too." They'd formed a network to protect her baby Andrew? Protect him from what dangers? The entire concept was incredible and frightening. "Surely we can settle this without making a major production out of it. Not everyone in the government is like Bardot."

"I realize that." He pushed back his chair and stood up. "Suppose we talk about it later. It's time we were on our way."

"You're being very evasive."

"Yes, I am. I want you to think about the problem before we discuss it."

She smiled shakily. "I don't like the sound of that. Are you keeping me in the dark again?"

He shook his head. "I won't deny I have a plan, but I won't do anything without your consent. It's too important a decision to be forced."

"And what would your wonderful council say to your generous gesture?"

"I don't give a damn what they say. This is between you and me." He paused. "And Andrew. We have to consider what's best for Andrew, Beth."

"Do you think I don't know that?" She turned away with a jerky movement. "You're right, we'll talk about it later. Serena said we should help ourselves to a picnic lunch. I'd better get busy packing it, hadn't I?"

"Beth." Jon's voice was soft with tenderness.

"*No*, I don't want to talk about it." Her hands were shaking as she opened the refrigerator door. "Not now."

His hands clenched slowly at his sides in helpless frustration as he watched her pull out the plastic cold cuts container. They had become too close the night before for him not to be able to read signs of sorrow and rejection in her expression. She was already considering the problem, and perhaps she had grasped tendrils of his solution on a subconscious level. It was difficult to keep up a barrier during a joining. He wanted to take her in his arms and help her, soothe away all the pain she would ever know, but he knew she wouldn't accept comfort now. He could only stand and wait until she was ready to come to him. He stepped forward and took the container. "Here, let me help you." Let me shoulder all your burdens, protect you from harm, smooth every rock-strewn path. "Did Serena tell you where she keeps the bread?"

Nine

"Sorry about the motel. I know it's not the Ritz, but I thought it was better for us to stay away from any of the large, well-known hotels in downtown Rochester." Jon leaned against the door that connected their adjoining rooms. "We have to keep a low profile until Gunner contacts us tomorrow morning."

"The motel's fine." Elizabeth went to the window and drew the beige print drapes, blocking out the early evening darkness. "Hotels are all pretty much the same, and at least this place is spotlessly clean. Do you suppose we can order from room service?"

"I doubt it. Why don't you shower and rest for a while, and I'll see what I can arrange as far as carry-out food goes? I saw a pizza parlor and a Mexican restaurant a few blocks from here. Do you have any preference?"

"Mexican."

He nodded as he turned away. "Mexican it is. Fasten the chain lock behind me. I'll knock when I come back."

"Are all these precautions necessary? I don't think we were followed. I didn't see anyone on the road."

"I didn't either." A thoughtful frown knotted his brow. "If they were good at their job, we wouldn't have seen them. It doesn't hurt to be careful."

She nibbled nervously on her lower lip. "Do you really think Gunner got away? I was so relieved when Bardot first told me about his men disappearing, I just jumped to that conclusion. What if something happened to their mobile phone, and they didn't really disappear? What if they were following Gunner and overtook him later?"

He glanced over his shoulder with an amused smile. "You're full of what-ifs tonight. I said I wanted you to think, not worry. Will it make you feel better if I swear there was no way those men could stop Gunner?"

"Not unless you tell me how you can be so sure."

"There are times when I could do without your Yankee show-me mentality." He held up his hands in mock surrender. "I'll tell you why I'm so sure later. During dinner. Okay?"

"Okay."

She watched the door close behind him and then obediently crossed the room to fasten the chain lock. She switched on the light, picked up the suitcase Serena had packed for her, and put it on the bed. Though not very large, it was heavy. When she had unlatched and opened it, she understood why. Not only did it contain several pairs of jeans and several sweaters, but Serena had packed underthings and even a portable hair dryer and a plastic bag of toiletries. However, it wasn't the practicality of Serena's choices that attracted Elizabeth's attention, but the one garment that was wildly impractical and completely fabulous. The rich peach-colored satin of a negligee and matching robe glowed jewellike against the sturdy fabric of a pair of denim jeans. Elizabeth's hand reached out to stroke the satin fabric and discovered that there was a note pinned to it.

You'll notice there's not one bead or sequin to be found on the enclosed negligee, but every woman needs a bit of glamour occasionally. Don't argue, wear it. It's from a medieval collection I designed two seasons ago, and I always thought it made me look like Morgan le Fay. It will suit you much better.

Serena

Elizabeth lifted the robe from the suitcase and held it up. It was a magnificently romantic garment, and the color would look good on her. Jon had never seen her in anything so seductive.

Seductive. Elizabeth felt color rise in her cheeks. The word had come so naturally to her mind. Seduction. Was that what she intended tonight? Her hands tightened on the peach-colored fabric. She would never be beautiful, but in this sensuous garment she would come close. It would surround any woman in an aura of glamour. Why was she hesitating? Only that same morning she had bewailed the fact that she always appeared in such unflattering attire before Jon, and now she had been given the perfect remedy.

Elizabeth grinned as she draped the gown over her arm and picked up the hair dryer and the bag of toiletries. She turned and walked briskly toward the bathroom. Oh, yes, by all means, she definitely planned on seduction.

She looked as vibrantly feminine as one of Gunner's Sybras.

Jon felt his breath catch in his throat, and he had to tighten his grip on the boxes of food he held to keep them from falling to the floor. "Beautiful." *She* was beautiful. Her brown hair hung straight and shining past her shoulders, and her skin was as ripe and silky as a peach, reflecting the glowing shade of the satin which flowed around her in a sensuous cloud. The robe was loose and fluid, the sleeves enormously wide and graceful. The gown beneath it was also loose, with a low square neck that revealed the lush slopes of her upper breasts. "Serena's design?"

Elizabeth nodded as she took the boxes from him and stood back to allow him to enter. "Her medieval season. She said every woman needs a little glamour in her life. Do you like it?"

"Yes." He had trouble forcing out words from his dry throat. "Sybra."

She gazed at him in bewilderment. "What?"

"In Gunner's province in Garvania there was a social order of women who were dedicated only to the sensual pleasures. Every thought and action was aimed at increasing their desirability and sexual performance. They were called Sybras."

Elizabeth wrinkled her nose. "It sounds like a very boring life."

His lips twitched. "They didn't seem to find it boring, and I guarantee their partners never complained of ennui."

"Did you ever—" She broke off. She didn't want to know. She was feeling shy and insecure enough without knowing she would be competing with a bevy of sexual experts. She turned away and moved to stand by the round teak table near the window. "You were gone a long time. I was beginning to get worried."

"I had a few phone calls to make, and something was bothering me so I decided to check on it." He closed the door and locked it. "And I stopped to buy a bottle of wine. It's not a terrific year, but I thought you might appreciate a little touch of class with our take-out specials. Heaven knows neither our surroundings nor our dinner has any great degree of élan." He was scarcely aware of what he was saying. The silk moved and flowed against her body with her every movement. Her bare, shapely feet were visible from beneath the hem of her robe and, for some odd reason, their nudity was almost as arousing as the sight of her breasts jutting from the neckline of the gown.

His gaze followed her across the room. He took the bottle of wine and two wine glasses from the paper bag he still carried. "The man at the liquor store assured me this was Napa Valley's finest."

She looked up after setting the paper plates of rice, beans, and burritos on the table. "Who did you call?"

"Gunner, for one." He smiled as he met her surprised gaze. "I contacted him through our local man. I thought you'd feel better if I could tell you I'd spoken to him directly. Andrew's fine. He's eating well, sleeping well, and according to Gunner, he's enjoying Einstein enormously."

"Thank goodness." Elizabeth collapsed into a chair. She hadn't realized how frightened she'd been until now. "Where are they?"

"At a small hotel near Rochester. They'll be joining us tomorrow at noon."

"Wonderful." Her smile was so radiant, it made him catch his breath.

"Yes." He cleared his throat and forced himself to look away. He shrugged out of Dane's suede car coat and threw it on the bed, then seated himself opposite her at the table. His hands were trembling as he opened the wine, and he could feel her gaze on his face. "I told you they were all right."

"But how did Gunner get away from them? What happened to Bardot's men?"

"Bardot's men are on their way to San Diego."

Elizabeth gazed at him in bewilderment. "San Diego? What on earth are you talking about? Why would they go to San Diego?"

Jon didn't look at her as he poured the bubbling white wine into their glasses. "Because Gunner told them that Bardot had ordered them to go there. He also told them a top-security blackout was in effect, and they were not to use their mobile phone or try to contact anyone until they reached San Diego." He put the bottle down on the table. "According to Gunner, they should be driving through Colorado right now."

"Gunner told them. Why would they believe . . ." She stopped. "Hypnosis?"

He nodded. "Combined with telepathic command."

"Mind control. It's incredible," she whispered. "You can actually make them do things against their will? Can you make anyone do what you want them to?"

"Almost anyone. Gunner has an eighty-five percent success rate in mind control, and mine is a little higher." He met her gaze unflinchingly. "But it's only done in the most extreme cases. To use our abilities to subvert another person's will or trespass on their privacy breaks the raznal. In our group that's a crime punishable by death, and there are only a few men who have the right to issue the order to ignore the raznal."

"And you're one of them," she murmured dazedly. "Gunner said I couldn't imagine the power you wielded." She shivered. "I don't know if I like the idea of someone being able to make me do something I don't want to do. Not even you."

"I was afraid you'd feel like that." Jon's hand tightened on his glass. "I can't deny the power is there, but it will never be used without your permission. I don't know how to impress upon you the seriousness of breaking the raznal." He looked down at the wine in his glass. "Look, when we first discovered the power of our abilities it was like we owned a wonderful toy. We experimented and played with it and thought we had discovered all the answers. Just think of the potential, Beth. In medicine and psychiatry alone we could make miraculous steps. Then we discovered there was an ugly side to the power that we'd never dreamed about. Without controls, it could come close to destroying our humanity. Now we have controls, we have the raznal but we'll never let ourselves forget the time when we didn't. That's why we need to find a place where it's possible to study and develop greater constraints." He lifted his gaze to meet her own. "Why do you think I haven't removed Bardot from the scene? It would be a simple thing to do, but I'd have to break the raznal. I can't do that without trying every other possible means first."

"Yet you gave Gunner permission to break it."

"To protect Andrew. Not only because he was your child, but because he's our hope for tomorrow." He leaned forward, his voice vibrant with urgency. "The Clanad is very lonely, Beth. We don't want to be alone, but we are. It's going to be a long time before we can come forward and try to find our place in the world. There's bound to be distrust and doubt at first, before we effect a unity, and we're going to need to bridge that sea of distrust. Remember how you referred to the old covered bridge you love so much? You said it was the last bridge home. Well, that's what Andrew will be, Beth. He's the bridge between the past and the future, between what we are and what we can be, between the lonely road and home."

Elizabeth's lips were trembling as she tried to smile. "For Pete's sake, Andrew is only three weeks old. He's not a bridge to anywhere yet. And I'm not sure I don't hope you're wrong about his potential. I'd rather enjoy having a normal, happy-go-lucky son."

"Maybe we are wrong," he said gently. "At any rate, we'll try to keep him safe as long as possible. There's no reason he can't have a happy childhood."

She lifted the glass to her lips and took a small sip of wine. "You're damn right he will. I'll make very sure he does."

He smiled. She had responded better than he thought she would. He lifted his own glass in a toast. "*We'll* make sure he does."

She nodded, picked up her plastic fork and took a bite of her burrito. "I accept the correction. You're a very handy man to have around in a tight situation, Jon Sandell."

His lips curved in a smile. "Oh, I think you'll find me adequately satisfying in a 'tight' situation."

The color rose to her cheeks. His play on words was abundantly clear and totally unexpected. The change in his tone from persuasive to sensual in the space of seconds caught her off guard. She lowered her gaze to her plate. "I'm sure you will be."

He went still. "Is that an invitation?"

She didn't look at him. "I promised you there'd be another time."

"You're sure?" he asked hoarsely. "Please be sure, Beth. I can't take any more rejection."

"I'm sure." She could feel his gaze as it moved over her face, her throat, her breasts. She was afraid to look up, afraid of what she'd see in his eyes. The sexual tension had gone on too long.

She was trembling on the brink, anything could tip the balance and send her over the edge. "What does it take to seduce you, for heaven's sake? I may not be a Sybra but I'm certainly doing my level best to—Jon!"

Her chair crashed over behind her as he pulled her up into his arms. His lips were hard and hungry on her own, and she could feel the wild pounding of his heart through the clothing that separated them. "You want *me*? Not Mark, not any other man? Me?"

"You." The crisp cotton of his shirt was rubbing against her breasts with the harsh rise and fall of his chest, and she could scarcely speak. His hard muscular thighs pressed the silk of her gown against her hips. She could feel the heat his body emitted, and his arousal was as stark and primitive as the glazed expression of hunger on his face. Did she look like that too? His fingers tangled in her hair and he pulled her head back to gaze into her eyes. He searched and found what he was looking for, and his low guttural exclamation aroused her as much as the feeling of his body against her own.

"Do you know how long I've wanted you?" His lips were moving over her throat as he curved her body into the hollow of his hips. "I've been burning for so long I'm surprised there's anything left of me."

"I don't doubt there's something left," she said faintly. "You appear to be very . . . substantial."

"Understatement." His tongue licked delicately at the pulse in the hollow of her throat. She shivered. His fingers curled in her hair and he tugged gently. "Definitely an understatement. Don't you think it's time we got rid of this?" Her robe fell in a shimmering pool of material on the carpet. "And this."

His fingers slowly pulled the neckline of her gown down from her left shoulder. "You have lovely shoulders." He uncovered her other shoulder and stepped back to look at her. The peach-colored bodice barely crested the tips of her breasts, and he could see the dark outline of her nipples through the silk. The muscles of his stomach twisted. "I can't hold out very long." He pushed the material to her waist, revealing her breasts, their dark pink nipples distended and pointed in the lamp-light. "In fact, I can't hold out at all." With one quick jerk the gown fell to her feet. "Beth!"

He picked her up and carried her to the bed. The beige taffeta coverlet felt cool beneath her naked back. Lord, she needed to feel coolness. She was hot, tingling, rigid and yet melting. She watched dazedly as he quickly removed his clothes. He never took his gaze from her as he disrobed. He was lithe and lean, his deeply bronzed body corded with rippling muscles. The triangle of dark hair on his chest was soft and silky. Soft. The thatch was the only part of him that appeared soft. He was made up of hard, driving masculine force.

In an instant, he was beside her on the bed. His hands moved over her yearningly, exploringly. "Do I please you? I want to please you. Let me . . ." His hands parted her thighs and his fingers stroked her. She gave out a little cry and surged up against him.

"You like that? God, so do I. You'll like this too." His head bent and his warm tongue delicately stroked her nipple.

She shuddered.

"So sensitive. Are they sore, love?"

"Only a little." She was barely conscious of having uttered the words. She couldn't breathe. Her heart was pounding hard, fast, her chest became tighter with every second.

He was over her, nudging against her. His eyes were dark and smoky with need as they met her own. He came into her slowly, so slowly. His head bent to her breast as he moved with excruciating deliberateness within her. His lips parted and she felt his breath feathering her nipple. "Take from me," he said thickly. "And I will take from you." His mouth closed on her breast.

At the same time he plunged forward and she arched helplessly up to take him as he had bade her. She was half moaning, half sobbing, her nails digging into the biceps of his shoulders. Her head thrashed back and forth as the rhythm of their lovemaking escalated, deepened. His mouth shifted to her other breast. The muscles of his thighs hardened with tension as his fingers moved down to tug gently at the soft hair that guarded her womanhood. She obediently opened to take more but there was no more to take. "Jon . . ."

She was trembling. He was moving hard, fast, filling every part of her. She couldn't take enough. She had to take more. Her legs curled around his hips and she clenched fiercely.

He cried out softly and raised his head. His

cheeks were flushed, his face heavy with sensuality. "Beth, I can't . . ." He lifted her hips with his hands and drove deep. She inhaled sharply. He paused and looked down at her. The expression on his face was savagely joyous. "*Mine!*" He exploded into motion with a power so forceful it stunned her.

Near. It was so near. The tears streamed down her cheeks as she moved against him. Closer. Fire. Passion. Hunger. The feeling so intense she couldn't bear it. Then she didn't have to bear it any longer as the tension released in a blinding rhapsody of sensation.

Her breath came in little sobs, and she couldn't stop trembling. She wasn't alone. Jon was trembling too. His breathing was labored and his chest gleamed with perspiration in the lamplight. She reached out with her finger and gently outlined the hard muscles of his stomach. He looked down at her and smiled.

It was a beautiful smile and she smiled happily back at him. "You were right," she said huskily. "We're definitely sexually compatible. Two in a million you said?"

He nodded. "That's what the genetic scientists reported." His eyes twinkled. "And I think we've successfully verified their analysis." He lowered his head and kissed her on the lips with exquisite tenderness. He moved off her and stood up. "I'll be right back."

She raised herself up on one elbow. "Where are you going?"

"I'm going to shower and try to make myself as

seductive as possible for my lady as she did for me." He picked up her wineglass from the table, refilled it and carried it back to the bed. He bowed with graceful panache. "For you, my love. You might try to take a little catnap. It's going to be a very long night."

Ten

"Tell me about Garvania." Elizabeth's voice was soft and blurred with contentment. "Is it very beautiful?"

"I think it is, but then it's my home. I'd like you to see it. I want you to see the rust-colored sands of the Zumara Desert and the tropical jungles of Samaria. We have flowers there that will take your breath away. The colors are . . ." He shrugged. "There are no words to describe how beautiful a place it is."

"But no snow." Elizabeth nestled her cheek closer into the hollow of his shoulder.

"No snow. I'd never seen snow before I came here. It's certainly a sight I'm glad not to have missed. Everything in Garvania is bolder and brighter."

She lifted her head to look down at him. "Now you wait just a minute. If you want bold, I'll have to show you a waterfall called Niagara. And as for bright, our Painted Desert could probably give your Zumara a run for its money."

He chuckled. "I'd heard that Americans are very competitive. I assure you I meant no disparagement."

"Well, I hope not. You may be a little ahead of us in mental development, but I imagine we could teach you a few useful things."

"I don't doubt it. You've already taught me a number of things I didn't know before." His finger touched the tip of her uptilted nose. "Love, respect, passion. You're a wonderful teacher, Beth."

"Am I?" Her throat was tight with emotion. "I guess you've taught me a few lessons too. You're not so bad yourself."

"I'm glad you're beginning to appreciate my finer qualities." The smile faded from his face. "But there's something you should realize. Competitiveness isn't only an American trait. I'm exceptionally competitive, probably more competitive than anyone you've ever met. It nearly killed me when you were married to Mark. I'd never thought of myself as an obsessive man, but I suddenly found that I had at least one obsession. I studied the video- and audiotapes the committee brought me, and I fell in love for the first time in my life." He smiled grimly. "I didn't want to fall in love, but I couldn't seem to stop myself. I told the council I wanted you and was going after you. Then they told about Mark's medical condition. How the devil could I mess up a man's last few months of life? Even I couldn't go that far, so I decided to wait." His dark eyes gleamed fiercely in the lamplight. "Do you know what waiting did to me? Knowing he was married to you, touching you, listening to you laugh." He drew a deep, uneven breath. "I just wanted you to realize how I felt. You're mine now, and you're going to stay mine. I'm not going to let anyone take you away from me."

She felt suddenly uneasy. The obsessiveness he mentioned would have been clear even if he hadn't put it into words. She wanted to belong to him, but . . . She shrugged away her qualms. Their relationship was just beginning. They would work things out. She tried to add a light note to the conversation to relieve the intensity of the moment. "I suppose an ordinary person like me should be grateful to be considered worthy by your august committee. Personally, I think someone must have screwed up on their paperwork."

His face softened. "Do you? I know why they thought you'd be an asset." Courage, integrity, and a loving nature. She radiated warmth like a glowing fire. His finger brushed the curve of her cheek caressingly. "Freckles. They're very rare in Garvania since we have darker complexions. Naturally we wanted such a phenomenon to be reproduced in—ouch!" He extracted his finger from her mouth. "And you have very fine teeth too."

"Are they also rare in Garvania?"

"No, but your cannibalistic proclivities are."

"Well, what do you expect? You'll find Americans are basically a very primitive people. We enjoy the simple things in life. A warm fire, a good meal, a secure place to—" She stopped and the laughter abruptly disappeared from her face as she finished—"come home to." Her cheek returned to its former place on his shoulder and she curled closer. "Hold me. I want you to hold me."

"Delighted." His arms went immediately around her. There was silence in the room. His hand moved up to gently message the tense muscles at the nape of her neck. "Something's bothering you."

"Yes."

"Do you want to talk about it?"

"No, but I guess we'd better. You said you had a plan for Andrew. Your plan doesn't include Mill Cottage, does it?"

"No."

She expelled her breath shakily. "I didn't think so."

"We've decided Andrew would be safer outside the United States."

"Why? Surely he'd be safer here. We have more freedom than any other country in the world."

"I'm not disputing that fact, but living in a free country may not be to Andrew's advantage. Democracy is based on a system of checks and balances, which breeds bureaucracy. Do I have to tell you how slow a bureaucracy moves? I don't doubt Bardot's agency will eventually be evaluated and eliminated, but it may take a long time. What if Andrew's uniqueness is discovered and popular opinion turns against him?"

"Where do you want him to go?"

"Have you heard of a country called Sedikhan?"

"It's an oil-rich sheikdom in the Middle East, isn't it?"

Jon nodded. "Sedikhan is ruled by Alex Ben Raschid, who is very democratic and devoted to his country's welfare." He paused. "But an absolute monarchy exists there, which means that once under Raschid's protection Andrew would be safe."

"I see."

"The sheik has agreed to accept the responsibility of keeping us all out of danger and will send his private plane to a small airport north of Rochester tomorrow evening."

"Sedikhan. It sounds so . . . foreign."

"It's a wonderful place to live. Andrew will love Sedikhan."

"How do you know that?" Her tone was suddenly fierce. "How can you be certain he'd be happier there than at Mill Cottage?"

"I can't tell you he'll be happier. I can only tell you I believe he'll be safer," Jon said quietly.

"The cottage is such a wonderful house for a child to grow up in." Elizabeth's voice was husky. "I love it so, Jon."

"I know you do." Jon's arms tightened around her. "I told you it would be your decision. If you decide to stay here, I'll make it work for us."

She experienced a jubilant flare of hope. "You will?"

"I will." He brushed the top of her head with his lips. "I've always wanted to live in a house with a paddle wheel."

"There are so many things there I'd like to show—" She broke off. "I'm not sure I want . . . Oh, Jon, I just don't *know*."

"Give yourself a chance to think things over. You don't have to make a decision this minute." He tilted her head up to look into her eyes. "In fact, I'd rather you directed your attention to other matters right now." He kissed her lightly. "If you're rested enough?"

"Again?" She grinned. "How polite you're being. You didn't ask me if I was too tired the last time, nor the time before that, nor—"

He placed two fingers on her lips to quiet her. "But this time I have something else in mind. It may be more tiring for you."

"Will I like it?"

He smiled lovingly. "Oh, yes, I don't think there's any question that you'll like it. I believe you enjoyed it very much the last time." He moved over her. "May I come in?"

Her eyes suddenly widened with understanding. "You mean . . . ?"

His brilliant dark eyes held her own as he slid slowly into her body. "Oh, yes, torches, my own love. Torches."

"I think he's grown," Elizabeth sighed blissfully as she cuddled Andrew closer. "I don't remember him weighing this much."

Jon chuckled. "May I point out you've only been separated a little over twenty-four hours? I doubt if he could have changed significantly."

"It seems like we've been apart much longer." So many things had happened in a short span of time. She had been bombarded by a dazzling barrage of ideas and emotions. Fear, sorrow, desire, love. "I believe I'm jealous, Gunner. Andrew's obviously perfectly content with you. After a little over three weeks of life I'm already expendable to him."

"He was only tolerating me," Gunner said with a grin. "He's really a ladies' man. He gets bored with members of his own sex after a while."

"From what Jon tells me he's not the only one who's a ladies' man," Elizabeth said lightly. "I'd be very curious to hear more about these Sybras."

"Now, I wonder how he came to mention Sybras," Gunner murmured, glancing sideways at Jon. "He couldn't have been making comparisons? If he was, it opens a whole new field of speculation. Was he comparing philosophical and cultural similarities, or erotic positions, or—"

"Gunner," Jon said warningly.

Gunner immediately subsided but there was a lingering glint of mischief in his eyes as he dropped the diaper bag he was carrying on the bed. "Like I said, I was only wondering. You know what an inquiring mind I have."

"I know very well." Jon's tone was dry. "Did you, by any chance, direct your inquisitiveness toward our departure arrangements for this evening?"

Gunner nodded. "Clancy Donahue will arrive in Raschid's private plane at Lindberg airport at five o'clock this afternoon." He glanced at his watch. "That's four hours from now. He asked us to be ready to leave by six. Donahue wants to arrive back in Marasef by tomorrow morning." He turned to Elizabeth. "He's arranged for you to stay with his wife, Lisa, and their son, at his residence in the Sedikhan desert for a week or two. He said to tell you his wife extends her personal invitation along with his own. She'll be delighted to have your company while her husband arranges your permanent quarters. Her son is only a year old, so you should have quite a bit in common."

"That's very kind of her." A troubled frown knitted Elizabeth's brow. She had been trying not to think of the decision Jon had burdened her with. Only five hours. She wasn't ready to make a decision of major importance. It was too soon. Leaving her home meant too much to her for her to rush into a commitment without giving the situation proper thought.

"The decision isn't with whom Elizabeth will stay when she goes to Sedikhan," Jon said quietly. "It's whether we'll be going at all. She may decide to stay in the United States."

Gunner's eyes widened. "But you said it wouldn't be . . ." He stopped as he met Jon's gaze. "I see. Well then, I'd better radio Donahue and inform him that we may not be leaving." He turned toward the door. "I'll go directly to the airport, and you can reach me there once Elizabeth has made her decision."

"Wait." Jon picked up his jacket from the chair. "I'll walk you to the truck. I need to use the mobile phone to call Barnett, and there are a few details I need to discuss with you." He smiled reassuringly at Elizabeth. "I'll be right back, love."

She nodded. "You don't have to hurry. I have to change Andrew anyway."

"You'll find a new brand of powder in the diaper bag. I bought it yesterday at a drugstore. It works better than your talc," Gunner said as he opened the door. "And the cream is in the— "

"She'll find it," Jon said impatiently. "You can discuss the merits of baby powder later. I need to contact Barnett as soon as possible."

"Jon obviously doesn't understand the importance of these matters." Gunner made a face at

Elizabeth over his shoulder. "You'll like the powder," he managed to say before Jon whisked him out into the hall and firmly closed the door behind them.

She did like the powder. When Andrew was freshly diapered, he smelled as deliciously fragrant and clean as only a baby can.

He was so beautiful. Was he smiling at her? Babies his age weren't supposed to smile, but she could swear he was grinning up at her. What do the authors of baby books know anyway? She asked herself. Andrew was a happy, contented baby. Maybe he *was* smiling at her. Her index finger gently touched the corner of his mouth. The smile deepened and she felt a ridiculous surge of triumph.

The door opened behind her but she didn't look around. "Jon, I think he's smiling at me. Isn't that clever? Babies aren't supposed to smile at so young an age."

"Maybe he's a freak like his father."

Elizabeth's heart leaped with fear and then started pounding painfully hard. Oh, no, Bardot! She straightened slowly and turned to face him.

Bardot stood in the doorway gazing at her with a smile of satisfaction on his face. He pocketed a key as he stepped into the room. "We'll soon find out if he is or not. The farm has a staff of doctors on tap, and we'll know within a few hours if he's a freak."

Elizabeth drew a deep breath and tried to steady her voice. "I told you once not to speak disrespectfully about my son. He is *not* a freak, and there's no way I'm going to let you take him anywhere."

"You have no choice. Do you think your friends are going to help you? For superbrains they're pretty damn stupid." Bardot's lips curled contemptuously. "Did you think I'd be dumb enough to permit you to slip through my hands twice? I let you get away. I wanted the baby, too, and I knew you'd lead me to him. I planted a bug in your friend's car. We've been watching this motel since early yesterday evening waiting for the kid to show up."

No wonder they hadn't seen anyone on the road, Elizabeth thought dully. Bardot had been able to monitor their every move from a safe distance.

Bardot smiled. "As for your two friends, we saw them leave the building, and I sent my men after them. I think six men against two should be enough to overpower them." He drew a pistol and pointed it at the baby lying on the bed. "And I don't think you're going to give me any trouble at all, are you?"

"He's only a baby," she whispered. She felt sick with horror. "No one would hurt a baby."

"No? Try me." His smile deepened. "But you won't take the chance, will you?"

"No." She turned back to Andrew and began to wrap him in a blanket. "I think you're sick enough to do it."

"Sick." He repeated the word as if it left a sour taste in his mouth. "You're a fine one to talk, with all your weird friends. Did you ever happen to think that they may be using you?"

"No."

"If Sandell and Nilsen are as smart as our scientists think they are, how do you expect to keep up? The two of them are bound to leave you far behind. They're going to leave us all behind. Pretty soon they'll be looking down their noses at us and—"

"That's enough, Bardot."

"What the hell!" Bardot whirled to face the two men standing behind him, his hand tightening on his gun. "You're not supposed to be here. What did you do to my men?"

"They're not hurt." Jon was calm, almost casual. "As a matter of fact, they're waiting for you in your car."

"Waiting? You're lying." Bardot shrugged. "Well, it doesn't matter whether you are or not. We'll just go down and see." He gestured with the gun. "After you."

"I don't think so. I'm afraid I've lost patience with you, Bardot."

"Do you want me to handle him?" Gunner asked with dangerous softness. "I'd be glad to take care of it. I don't like bastards who threaten to shoot children."

"No." Jon's eyes were glinting fiercely. "Oh, no. He's mine."

Bardot turned suddenly so the range of his pistol encompassed Elizabeth and Andrew. "You're crazy. In case you didn't notice, I'm the one with the gun. Do you think I won't use it?"

Elizabeth stepped forward to stand in front of Andrew. "Be careful, Jon. He actually would hurt Andrew. He's not normal."

Bardot's laugh was a harsh bark. "*I'm* not normal? You're the ones who aren't normal. Freaks. You're all freaks."

"That's not what you mean," Jon said quietly. "You say freaks, but you mean monsters. Give me the gun."

"The hell I will." His gun was aimed squarely at Elizabeth. "Come here," he said to her. "I don't think your friend will try anything if the barrel of my gun is pressed to your back."

"Put the gun down." Jon moved to face Bardot. "I don't want to do this, Bardot. We can still try to negotiate, if you'll be reasonable."

"Stay right where you are." Bardot's tongue nervously moistened his lips. "Don't come any closer."

"I'm not coming any closer." Jon met his eyes. "Give up, Bardot."

"No!" Bardot began to curse stridently.

Jon slowly shook his head and said something in a tone too low for Elizabeth to understand.

"*Aiiii!*" Bardot dropped the gun, and he desperately tried to cover his face with his hands. He screamed again, and the agonized sound sent a chill down Elizabeth's spine. "No! Go away. No!" His words faded into a whimper as he sank to his knees.

Elizabeth stared at him in horror. "What's wrong with him?"

Bardot was curled into the corner beside the door, his hands still covering his eyes, like a child afraid of the dark. He was sobbing, muttering almost inaudibly. "Please. Go away."

"Bring Andrew, Gunner." Jon picked up Elizabeth's coat, draped it around her shoulders, and then picked up her suitcase. "We have to leave now, love."

Elizabeth felt as if she were frozen in place as she stared at Bardot. "What did you do to him?"

Jon's arm went around her as he gently propelled her from the room. "You don't have to worry about Bardot. I told his men to wait fifteen minutes and then come after him." He closed the door and led her down the corridor. "He won't be a danger to us any longer."

"You said something to him. I didn't hear what it was, but you said something."

"Yes."

"What was it? What did you say to him? *Tell* me, dammit!"

Jon's eyes were riveted straight ahead. "You heard him. He was a man who saw only ugliness all around him. I just told him what he saw was true."

Her eyes were opened wide and she had a stricken expression on her face as she waited for him to continue. "I have to know, Jon."

Jon still didn't look at her as he hurried her across the parking lot to the truck. Gunner was already fastening Andrew into the restraint seat. "I didn't say much. Only one word really."

"What?"

"Monsters."

Eleven

Elizabeth stood gazing at Jon as he opened the door of the truck for her. Monsters. How horrible it would be to have one's worst nightmares come true.

"For Pete's sake, stop looking at me like that," Jon said with scarcely contained ferocity. "Do you think I enjoyed doing what I did? I gave him every chance. He would have shot you and Andrew in the blink of an eye."

"I know."

A little of the tension he felt ebbed from him. "Look, it's not permanent. I suggested to Bardot's men that they'd been doubting their boss's stability for the past few months. When they find him like that, they'll assume he's had a breakdown. A few weeks from now I'll send a man to see Bardot, and the hallucination will disappear. He'll be entirely normal again." His lips twisted. "As normal as possible for a man with his kind of mind. His investigation will be discredited and we'll be safe." He paused. "For a little while. There's no guarantee the file on the Clanad won't be pulled out of the mothballs and opened again."

"You don't paint a very rosy picture."

"No, but it's an honest one." He met her gaze gravely. "I made you a promise. I'll never lie to you again."

It had started to snow, and the large flakes caught in Jon's dark hair and dusted his suede jacket with diamanté crystals. She had a fleeting memory of that night on the deck when he had stood looking at the falling snow with such eagerness and curiosity. He expressed the same enthusiasm and curiosity in regard to all his surroundings. He was totally brilliant and would become even more intelligent with each passing year. She felt a sudden surge of panic grip her heart. "Bardot said someday you'd leave me far behind."

Jon stiffened warily. "The man is an idiot. Beth, for heaven's sake, you know me better than that."

"Do I? I'm not sure about anything right now." She lifted her hand to rub her temple. "I have to think. Everything is going around in circles in my mind." She held out her hand. "Give me the keys to Serena's car."

"Where are you going?"

"I don't know. I may just drive around for a while. I have to straighten out my thoughts."

"Stay with me. We'll talk about it. I know what happened with Bardot frightened you." His hands slowly clenched at his sides. "I'm *not* what he called me. I'm neither a freak nor a monster. I'm a man who loves you." His voice was harsh with strain. "And that's what I'll be for the rest of our lives. Don't leave me, Beth."

His words were an entreaty from a proud man who found it almost impossible to plead. Even through the haze of bewilderment enveloping her, she was aware of the desperation in his plea.

She smiled tremulously. "I'm not running out on you. It seems as if I've been on the run since the moment I met you. It's about time I stopped running. I have a decision to make. Give me the keys, Jon."

He slowly reached into his pocket, drew out the key ring, and placed it in her palm. "I'll wait for you here."

She shook her head. "Go on to the airport and I'll meet you there later." Her hand suddenly closed on his arm. "Stop looking at me so suspiciously. I'm leaving Andrew with you, after all. Do you think I'd ever run out on him?"

She saw a flicker of pain cross his face before he smiled sadly. "No, you'd never leave Andrew." He stepped up into the truck. "Try not to be too long. I'll be waiting for you."

Clancy Donahue glanced at his watch. "It's nearly six o'clock. Do you think she's coming?"

"Of course she's coming." Jon stared out from the cockpit window at the falling snow. "Andrew is here."

The older man's keen blue eyes were gentle as they rested on Jon's face. "Funny thing about women, they pour out so much love to all the people they care about that you wouldn't think they'd have enough to go around." He smiled. "But somehow there's always enough."

"I'm not so sure."

"I am." Clancy nodded toward a car which was approaching the hangar several yards away. "Is that your Elizabeth?"

Jon felt the muscles in his stomach knot. Lord, he was afraid. "Yes, I'll go and meet her."

Clancy nodded. "You'd better hurry. My flight plan requires me to leave here in a few minutes."

"She may have decided not to go."

Clancy shrugged. "The trip still wasn't wasted. We were able to make plans for smuggling the rest of the Clanad out of the U.S. during the next few months."

Jon smiled crookedly. "Sedikhan is going into the sanctuary business in a big way. I guess you know how grateful we are."

"You'll earn your keep. Alex will probably set up a brain trust and have you all slaving away from daybreak until dark." Clancy grinned. "You'll like Alex Ben Raschid. He's a tough man but he's absolutely fair."

"That's nice." Jon was no longer listening. He was watching Elizabeth as she got out of the car. "I'll be right back."

Elizabeth was halfway across the tarmac on the way to the plane when he reached her. The light streaming from the open doors of the hangar glinted on her rich brown hair and revealed the paleness of her grave face.

"You cut it close." Jon cleared his throat. "I was getting worried, it's snowing pretty hard now."

"I had a lot to think about." Her thoughts had been so clear when she had parked the car at the hangar, but now she was having a problem saying what she felt. "And I had trouble finding the airfield. It's certainly out in the boondocks."

"That's the reason we chose it." His jaw squared and he drew a deep breath. "I've been doing some thinking, too, and I'm not going to let you go. No matter what you've decided, I still know we can work things out. Our problems aren't insurmountable, for Pete's sake. We'll go back to the cottage with Andrew and be married. I can make you happy. I may not be Mark but—"

"Stop right there," Elizabeth said crisply. "I think we'd better clear up that point before we go any further. No, you're not Mark Ramsey. You're not as handsome, or as gentle, and certainly not as easy to get along with."

Jon scowled. "You don't have to tell me that. I know how you felt about Mark. Well, give me time and . . ."

"Jon, will you be quiet," she said. "I'm trying to make a declaration and you're making it very difficult. Mark was wonderful, and I loved him very much. He was my first love, which is something quite special. You say I belong to you, but you have to realize you can't possess the part of me that was married to Mark Ramsey. You can't have my past, it belongs to me." She smiled shakily. "But my present and my future are yours."

"I'll take them," he said instantly.

"Not yet. I'm not finished." She shook her head reprovingly. "Once you accused me of being easy. Aren't you even going to ask if I love you?"

"I'm afraid to ask," he said simply.

She felt tears sting her eyes and tenderness tighten her throat. "Oh, Jon." She took a quick step forward and came into his arms. "I love you so much it's killing me. Why do you think I fought against it for so long? I knew as soon as I let you into my life my peaceful existence would fly out the window."

"You love me?" His words were muffled in her hair. "It's not just sexual attraction? You really love me?"

"You're a difficult man to convince." Her arms tightened around him. "I *love* you. It's not first love, but it's just as deep, perhaps deeper. I realize now that nothing in our lives is permanent. We grow and change all the time, and I think the ways in which we love must change and grow too. Oh, I don't know if I'm making any sense. But I do know you're the most important person in my life."

"You won't be sorry, Beth. I'll take such good care of you. I'll take you home to Mill Cottage and—"

"No."

He lifted his head. "What?"

"No, we're not going to Mill Cottage." She forced herself to smile. "We're going to Sedikhan."

Jon's gaze searched her face. "Not if it's going to make you unhappy. I told you I could make it work here."

She shook her head. "No, it will be safer for you and Andrew in Sedikhan. I decided I couldn't live with myself if I were that selfish. I don't deny it's going to hurt to leave. It's going to hurt like hell, but sometimes a person has to give up one love to gain another. You said Andrew was a bridge between the past and the future. Well, there are other bridges. I think love can be a bridge. I'm not afraid of what you are or what you'll become. I have enough to worry about living up to my own potential, without going into a panic about yours. After all, determination and initiative count for something too. I figure I can give you a run for your money regardless of your IQ."

"I don't doubt it." Jon's eyes were warmly tender. "I'll probably have to watch out or I'll be left at the gate, my dear Yankee."

She reached up to frame his face in her two hands and look into his eyes. "I love you with all my heart, but that love won't be the last bridge home. Because it *is* home. Wherever we are together will be home."

His dark eyes were glittering. "I'll bring you back to Mill Cottage someday. I promise you, Beth."

"Perhaps by that time Sedikhan will be home, and I'll only want to come for a visit. I'm sure the first generation of Cartwrights had moments of homesickness for the old country when they first built Mill Cottage." She smiled. "We Yankees are very adaptable once we put our minds to it."

He turned his head to press his lips to her palm. "May I say I'm very happy this particular Yankee happened into my life? Lord, I love you, Beth. You'll see, I'll make you so damn happy you'll never think of Mark Ra—" He broke off as he met her eyes. "Sorry. I told you I was competitive. I guess it's going to take a little time." A sudden joyous smile lit his face. "But we've got time, haven't we?" He kissed her with a wild exuberance. "We've got the rest of our lives."

"The rest of our lives," she repeated softly. Joy, hope, beauty. They had so much together it would soon crowd out any lingering sadness.

"Your hair is getting damp." He brushed away a snowflake that was clinging to her temple. "I'd better get you into the plane." He still didn't move. "I don't want to let you go. Why the hell do we seem to spend all our time surrounded by snow?"

"I guess it's the penalty you must pay for falling in love with a Yankee." She grinned and stepped back. "I remember one or two occasions that weren't too uncomfortable, and I'm looking forward to many, many more." She linked her arm through his. "But I guess we'd better go inside. Your Mr. Donahue will be getting impatient."

Gunner met them at the door and handed her a towel. "I thought you might need this." He raised an eyebrow at Jon. "Remind me to give you a few pointers. I understand snow tends to dampen a lady's ardor." He turned back to Elizabeth and his face softened as he saw her glowing eyes. "But, on the other hand, I could be wrong. Maybe it works as an aphrodisiac for a special few. Let me help you with your coat, Elizabeth. We're going to Sedikhan?"

"We're going to Sedikhan." She dabbed at her cheeks and hair with the towel.

"I'd better go to the cockpit and let Clancy know it's all right to take off." Jon brushed her temple with his lips. "I'll be back as soon as we're airborne, love." He turned away. "See that she and

Andrew are properly buckled up and comfortable, Gunner."

"Right." Gunner motioned across the luxurious cabin to one of the deep blue plush chairs by the window. "If you'll sit down, I'll bring Andrew to you. I have to run out to the truck and get his restraint seat. I didn't want to set it up in the plane until I was sure we were going."

A few minutes later she was holding sweet, warm Andrew and gazing out the window at the rapidly falling snow. She was leaving. It might be years before she saw the beloved familiar landscape of her country again. For an instant she felt a poignant sense of loss, but she firmly crushed it down. No one ever has everything he or she wants, and she had so much to be grateful for. She had Jon and Andrew and Gunner. Love and friendship and purpose. Yes, she was very lucky.

She leaned back in the chair and closed her eyes, her arms tightening around Andrew. She wouldn't look out the window again until they were high above the clouds, until they had left her home far behind. It would be easier that way. She knew she would be all right after the initial homesickness wore off, but she couldn't deny the pain she felt. She only hoped Jon would stay up front with Donahue until she could get herself under control. He would want to share her pain, and she mustn't let him see how difficult leaving home was for her.

She would try to think of something else. Something that would take her mind off all she was leaving behind. She would think of the warm deserts of Sedikhan, Jon's smile of delight before he kissed her, the exquisite scent of lilacs, the mist-laden meadows lit by beautiful glowing torches.

So beautiful. So familiar. Returning once again to lighten her spirit and dispense the dark desolation of the moment with warm understanding and love. A loving balm soothing away her sorrow and showing her a brighter tomorrow. Such wonderful torches . . .

Torches!

But that meant . . . The realization jarred her from her haze of contentment. But how? Jon was in the cockpit with Clancy Donahue, and Gunner had left the plane to bring the restraint seat from the truck.

Slowly, very slowly, Elizabeth opened her eyes.

Andrew was smiling at her.

THE EDITOR'S CORNER

Next month is an important landmark for all of us on the LOVESWEPT team—our fourth birthday! I received an absolutely wonderful letter a few months ago, and I decided to wait until now to share it with you, because its message is a real birthday tribute to LOVESWEPT. The letter came from a woman and her husband who have been married a long time. He is enthusiastic about televised sports; she is a romance reader who counts LOVESWEPT her favorite line. One Sunday afternoon while he was engrossed watching a game, his wife sat nearby reading a LOVESWEPT and chuckling and laughing aloud at various passages. Fortunately, her husband didn't get annoyed, only curious, and later that night he asked if he could borrow the book she had so obviously enjoyed. She loaned it to him. He loved it. He asked to read more of those "terrific stories." Their letter—a joint effort—thanked us not only for entertaining them so much, but also for helping to put a whole lot of new zing and zip into their relationship. I treasure this letter, as I treasure so many you've written to me through the years.

So what do we have for you on our birthday month? An especially merry—perhaps inspiring?—quartet of romances.

First, in talented Joan Elliott Pickart's **WILD POPPIES**, LOVESWEPT #190, you'll encounter a simply delightful couple. Heroine Courtney Marshall, a lovely young widow, decides she must go on a husband hunt to provide her two small children with a sweet, reliable father. Luke Hamilton is a gorgeous hunk of man who doesn't appear to be the least bit steady to Courtney so she immediately rules him out and tells him the reason! Luke is floored by Courtney's "quest" and more than a little worried about the fate of such a beautiful and innocent soul out there in the woods with all those big, bad wolves. (And Luke should

(continued)

know—he has howled with the best of them!) Protecting and pleasing Courtney are priorities for Luke that soon turn to fiery passion in this love story whose charms will linger with you for many a day.

Who would guess that behind the pretty face, just under the lovely blond hair of Iris Johansen lurks a whole universe of people, places, adventures, and love with all its joys and a few of its sorrows? A stranger wouldn't guess but all of us know, right? And next month Iris will tour you through places you've visited with her before and she'll reacquaint you with a few old friends while she delights you anew with a marvelous romance, **ACROSS THE RIVER OF YESTERDAY,** LOVESWEPT #191. Part cowboy, part cavalier, and all man, Gideon Brandt knew his footloose days were numbered the very second he saw violet-eyed Serena Spaulding. But Serena was bound to others by secrets and responsibilities that forced her to hide from Gideon for years. He'd searched the wide world for her . . . and when he recaptured her at last it was hardly the ideal place or time for a love to flourish. Yet, even as their very lives were threatened, their desire for each other blazed to white heat . . . a sensational love story!

Witty, whimsical, passionate are the words that readily describe **THE JOY BUS,** LOVESWEPT #192, by the very creative Peggy Webb. Ms. Jessie Wentworth, mistress of all she surveys and a workaholic of the first order, is alternately baffled and beguiled by devastatingly handsome Blake Montgomery. Blake is a professor using his sabbatical for meandering through the countryside and putting on the magic shows he finds such fun to do, all out of his pink touring bus! Wonderfully down to earth—and earthy!—Blake makes Jessie see stars—and even wish on them. But how could she be sure that their love for one another wasn't just another illusion? JOY BUS is—truly—a joy!

(continued)

The book Kay Harper has created for you for next month is so fast-paced, so full of surprises, so breath-taking in the passionate intensity of its romance, that the best place for you to read it would be in a plane because you'd have a seat belt and a ready supply of pure oxygen! Find the next best spot to settle in and fly away even without a plane with **RAVEN ON THE WING**, LOVESWEPT #193. The hero is a man you know very well from **IN SERENA'S WEB**, LOVESWEPT #189 this month. Joshua Long avoids brunettes as if they carried the plague, as you'll recall. He will only date blondes and Serena has clued us into the reason: Josh knows the woman of his dreams will be a brunette . . . and she'll put an end to his playboy days. His intuition was right. He meets his loving fate in the sexy shape of Raven Anderson, a woman as beautiful as she is enigmatic. When the maddeningly mysterious Raven disappears, Josh has to use all the formidable tools he can bring to hand . . . and in the process almost destroys the woman he only wants to cherish. This is a riveting love story!

I hope that in the year to come not one of our LOVESWEPTS will disappoint you.

Warm regards,

Carolyn Nichols

Carolyn Nichols
   Editor
LOVESWEPT
Bantam Books, Inc.
666 Fifth Avenue
New York, NY 10103